MIRACLES

BEST-SELLING BOOKS
by TERRI BLACKSTOCK

MIRACLES

Includes Two Complete Novels

THE LISTENER THE GIFTED

TERRI BLACKSTOCK

THOMAS NELSON
Since 1798

NASHVILLE   DALLAS   MEXICO CITY   RIO DE JANEIRO   BEIJING

Published in Nashville, Tennessee, by Thomas Nelson. Thomas Nelson is a registered trademark of Thomas Nelson, Inc.

Published in association with Alive Communications, Inc., 7680 Goddard Street, Suite 200, Colorado Springs, CO 80920.

Thomas Nelson, Inc., titles may be purchased in bulk for educational, business, fund-raising, or sales promotional use. For information, please e-mail SpecialMarkets@ThomasNelson.com.

Scripture quotations in *The Listener* are from The Holy Bible, New International Version (NIV). © 1973, 1978, 1984 by International Bible Society. Used by permission of Zondervan Publishing House. All rights reserved.

Scripture quotations in *The Gifted* are from the New American Standard Bible ® (NASB). © 1960, 1977, 1995 by The Lockman Foundation. Used by permission. All rights reserved.

This book is a work of fiction. Names, characters, places, and incidents are either the products of the author's imagination or are used fictitiously. Any resemblance to actual persons, living or dead, events, organizations, or locales is entirely coincidental and beyond the intent of the author or publisher.

ISBN: 978-1-59554-511-4

Printed in the United States of America
08 09 10 11 RRD 5 4

the Listener

At this, the man's ears were opened, his tongue was loosened and he began to speak plainly.

MARK 7:35

FOREWORD

My friend Terri Blackstock has written a simple yet profound story with a vital message.

First, though, I want to say how I rejoice that *The Listener's* royalties all go to a great cause, Samaritan's Purse, an agency that gives people food, clothes, help, and the good news about Jesus Christ. You can read Terri's heart by her choice to lay up her treasures in heaven, not on earth. She is living out the book's vision by recognizing people's deepest needs and reaching out to help them in the name of Jesus. May the rest of us do the same.

We are all made for a person and a place. Jesus is the person. Heaven is the place. As Christians our lives and our words should draw others to what they desperately need. As we see in *The Listener,* we must become more alert to the people around us, realizing the Jesus we have is the Jesus they need.

While reading this book, I thought about how God hears the heart cries of all people everywhere, every moment. Jesus went to the cross to deliver us from our suffering. His eternally scarred hands and feet proclaim how expensive and valuable His gift is. We must first come to grips with this, and only then will others see it through us.

Terri captures the fact that it isn't just other people who are missing out on what we have to offer them. It's we who are missing out on the joy of being used by God. We need to share Jesus as much as people need to hear about Him.

If your Christian life is boring, this book offers a cure. Disciples live on the edge, asking, "How can I serve you today, Lord? Who can I touch for you?" And at the end of the day they can pray, "Thanks for using me, Jesus." They don't think about the day's sacrifices. They think about the sheer joy of being used by God to touch the lives of others—to meet their needs, love them and share the truth about Jesus through their actions and their words. When Jesus said, "It's more blessed to give than to receive," he wasn't kidding!

As we see in *The Listener*, every day people with great needs pass beneath our radar. We need to change our radar setting and learn to see those people and their needs. Neighbors, coworkers, parents we sit by at our kids' games, the mail carrier, bus driver, grocery checker, pizza guy, UPS delivery person . . . they all need Jesus. They need to hear us say, "Taste and see that the Lord is good." (I have a friend who regularly says to telemarketers, "I will listen to what you have to say, if when you're done you'll listen to something very important I'd like to tell you." They almost always agree, and he shares the gospel. Even annoying interruptions can be divine appointments!)

I pray that through reading Terri's book, many will be inspired to listen to the cries—even the silent ones—of people all around us who need to know Jesus. And may we learn to treasure the privilege that's ours to tell people about the one we love, because he first loved us.

RANDY ALCORN

1

THE DREAM CAME ON A SUNDAY NIGHT, AFTER AN afternoon of golf and an evening of watching politicians debate on cable. Like some divine hand, it seemed to grab Sam Bennett by the collar and pull him under. As if he were trapped in front of a huge movie screen, he saw a woman in a tiny room with a tin roof and a dirt floor, searching desperately for something. She grabbed things down from cupboards, off of shelves, turned things over, removed the cushions from her couch, searched behind doors and under rugs. It was a frustrating dream, one that seemed to have no end, until finally, Sam saw a coin, carelessly dropped in the corner of the room. The woman in the dream saw it at the same time, and she fell on it and snatched it up and began to weep with joy.

One lousy coin? he thought. *Why would she be so excited over one lousy coin?* Restlessly, Sam turned over in his sleep and buried his face in his pillow. The words of his pastor's sermon earlier that day played over and over in his mind. Words about reaching a hurting world. About hearing people's spiritual needs. He hadn't even listened that hard when the preacher had uttered them, but now they came back to him like recorded phrases that reeled around and around and around in his head, refusing to leave him until they sank in.

And then he heard the voice, the voice that woke him as it reverberated through his mind with holy power. "Ephphatha! Ephphatha!" He sat upright in bed.

The word vibrated through him, though he didn't know its meaning. It was Hebrew, he thought. Or, perhaps, Greek. And whose was the voice?

He was wide awake now, drenched in a cold sweat, and he was trembling. Kate, his wife, lay next to him, undisturbed. Quietly, he got out of bed and stumbled through the house. He went to the kitchen sink and splashed water on his face, then headed for the comfort and refuge of his recliner. It was four o'clock in the morning, too early to be up, yet he couldn't go back to sleep. It wasn't the dream that disturbed him so much, but the voice. It had had such power, such authority.

Ephphatha! What did it mean? Now that he thought of it, he was sure the voice hadn't been a part of the dream. He had only seen the woman, the coin in his sleep. No, the voice had the authority of God. Could the Lord have spoken to him tonight? But why would he speak in another language? Why would God utter something that so disturbed his spirit, something resonating with importance, but something he wasn't able to understand? Was it some kind of sign, or was he just losing it?

He took a deep breath and tried to shake the cobwebs out of his brain. The thought of going back to bed and facing more of the same was out of the question, so he finally put on a pot of coffee. After it had brewed, he poured a cup, then sat there sipping on it, trying to decide if the dream was something he should give more thought, or if he should dismiss it altogether.

Did it have something to do with the sermon he had yawned through yesterday? John, the pastor, had been waxing eloquent about the lost sheep. Something about leaving ninety-nine to go after one.

Sam had been more interested in the second hand on his watch. He'd figured if John didn't wind down soon, there would be a ridiculous line at every restaurant in town.

Was that why he'd had the dream? Did that word, *Ephphatha*, contain some kind of rebuke about listening in church? Now that he thought about it, John had been on a roll yesterday. By the end of the sermon, his face was reddening and he was leaning over the pulpit, shaking his hands to make his point. Sam hadn't seen John that worked up since he'd given his life to ministry during their sophomore year of college. Back then, John had often gotten red-faced and loud when he tried to change the hearts of Sam and his friends.

Sam had hoped it wouldn't mean that John would give a long, drawn-out benediction, then have them sing all four verses of the final hymn, while the Presbyterians got to the restaurants first.

"Have you ever considered what God hears in the hearts of people?" the pastor had asked. "What spiritual needs cry out to him? What if we could hear with God's ears?" Then he had looked around the sanctuary at the faces one by one. His eyes had met Sam's, and Sam tried to look more awake. He felt guilty when he saw disappointment cross over John's face.

"Most of you don't even hear with the ears you have," the pastor said in a duller voice. "Your ears are clogged up, and you can't hear the most obvious things. So there are people with needs out there just crying to be met, yet so few of God's laborers are going out to rescue them. If you want to hear, if you want to truly see, come to the altar now. Get on your knees and ask God to use you."

If God was mad at him now, Sam thought, it was because of his attitude yesterday. Sam had checked his watch again. He remembered thinking that if anyone went to that altar during the first verse and ripped out a quick prayer of commitment, they might still get out of there by twelve. If no one came, they might wind down after the second verse. But after the second verse, the pastor had nodded to the choir director to keep the song going. He said that he knew there was someone out there who felt the Holy Spirit calling, and he didn't want to close the service until they did their business with God.

Sam had actually considered going himself, just to wrap things up.

When no one responded, the pastor finally gave up and brought the service to an end. Sam hadn't wasted any time grabbing his wife's hand, making his way out of the pew, and pushing through the crowd to the exit door. He hadn't given the sermon another thought.

Now he tried to sort back through the points in that sermon. Was there something there about lost coins? Had John mentioned that unknown word? Had all of it somehow gotten snagged in his consciousness, even though he couldn't remember it now?

He was still trying to understand the dream when Kate got up some time later. "You're up early," she said.

He sipped his coffee. "Couldn't sleep."

"Was I stealing the covers?"

"No. I just had some dreams."

"Bad ones?"

He shrugged. "No, not really. Just weird stuff. You know the kind. Something's lost and you can't find it."

"I have those dreams," Kate said, her sleepy eyes widening. "I'm running through the airport to catch a plane, but I can't seem to make the gate. Or I'm in college and I'm trying to get to my final exam, only I haven't been to class all semester and don't know where the room is. Or I have to speak to a room full of people, and I look down and realize I'm still in my pajamas—"

"It wasn't like that," he cut in, irritated. "It was a little scarier."

"Scary? Why?"

He frowned. "I don't know. I'm not sure."

She considered that for a moment. "I have scary dreams sometimes too. The ones where someone's about to hurt me, but I can't scream." She poured herself a cup of coffee, then remembered another one. "Or the one where someone's throwing matches at me, but I can't put them out . . ."

He gazed at his wife. "Kate, have you thought of getting psychiatric help?"

"Hey, you're the one who couldn't sleep last night. I slept like a baby." She brought the cup to her lips.

"I want to be useful."

He frowned at the out-of-context comment, then decided that she meant it in regard to his dreams. "Don't worry about me." He got up and stretched. "Guess I'll go take my shower."

By the time he had showered and dressed, he was feeling a little better. The dream was just a dream, he thought, just a collage of images and phrases that he'd heard in the last few days. The preacher's message, something they'd talked about in Sunday school, maybe something he'd overheard subconsciously. It didn't matter. It had all mixed together in some kind of virus of thoughts, and his brain was just coughing it up as he slept. There was nothing to worry about.

2

AFTER HE'D TAKEN KATE TO WORK AT THE HOSPITAL, he parked in front of the diner across the street. Kate wasn't a breakfast eater, but he liked the works. Years ago, when they still had children at home, they had settled into a routine of drinking coffee together in the mornings, then going their separate ways. Now, when she headed for the hospital at seven, he headed for the diner to eat breakfast.

Still a little more unsettled than he wanted to admit, he went into the diner and took a seat at the counter. The popular place was loud with barely controlled chaos that always got his adrenaline pumping. In the front, irritable waitresses yelled orders to each other, and occasionally Sam could hear Leon, the cook in the back, let out a stream of curses that made Sam consider swearing the place off. But he always came back. Nowhere else could he get his eggs cooked exactly right.

He picked up the newspaper someone had left on the counter and scanned the headlines. Janie, his regular waitress, looked distracted as she approached him. "Morning, Sam. You're a little early today."

"Yeah," he muttered without looking up, "I had trouble sleeping."

"A little rest could change my whole life."

Now he looked up at her. She looked tired and had circles under her eyes and wrinkles he hadn't noticed before. He wondered how old she was. Forty? Forty-five? "Yeah? You can't sleep, either?" he asked.

She frowned and gazed across the counter. "Huh?"

"What you said about rest."

Her eyes narrowed. "Sam, all I said is that you're here early this morning. You sure you're all right?"

He stared at her for a moment. Hadn't he heard her say something about rest? He shook his head. "Whatever. I'll take the usual."

He watched, perplexed, as she went to yell his order to the angry cook.

The voice of the woman sitting two stools down from him distracted him from Janie. "Gravity's just gonna let go of me, and I'm gonna go flying out into the universe."

Amused, Sam glanced over at her. "That's a new variation on the 'stop the world I want to get off' theme."

Startled, the woman looked up at him. "What is?"

His grin faded. "I'm sorry. I thought you were talking to me."

She touched her hair with a shaky hand. "I didn't say anything."

"Oh," he said, "sorry." He forced himself to look back down at the newspaper. After a second, he heard the voice again.

"I'm gonna hurl out into the universe and no one will notice I'm gone." He looked at the woman again. She had tears in her eyes, and he knew without a doubt that the hopeless words had come from her.

He cleared his throat and leaned toward her. "That time . . . were you talking to me?"

She looked annoyed. "I wasn't talking to anyone. I'm just sitting here minding my own business."

He was getting aggravated. Who was she trying to kid? He was positive he'd heard her. "You didn't *say* anything?"

"No!"

Janie came back with his breakfast just as the woman belted out the denial. "Sam, you're not causing trouble with our other customers, are you?" she asked with a wink.

He shook his head. The woman was giving him the creeps. "I must be hearing things. Look, I think I'll go sit at that table."

Janie nodded, so he stuffed the paper under his arm, grabbed his plate and coffee, and moved over to the empty booth in the corner. He set his coffee down and slipped into his seat and began to eat. The place was filling up with nurses and medical students from the hospital across the street.

Normally, he saw the same faces every day, but he rarely spoke to any of them.

"There's just no point," the man at the table next to him said.

Sam looked over his shoulder. "In what?"

The man shot him a look. "Excuse me?"

"You said there's just no point. In what?"

The man looked shaken. "Uh . . . I must have been thinking out loud. Guess I'm farther gone than I thought. Sorry."

"It's okay," Sam said. "No biggie." He started to eat but the man spoke again.

"If I could just have more than a ten minute conversation . . . have somebody really listen . . . be heard . . ."

Sam looked up again, starting to get angry. What was this guy's problem? Why did he insist on pouring his heart out to Sam? But the man wasn't looking at him—he was staring down at his plate. The words were still coming, but his mouth wasn't moving.

"Everybody's always in a hurry. Nobody has time."

Slowly, Sam began to realize that the man wasn't speaking. Neither had the woman or Janie . . . He wasn't hearing audible words or voices, although they sure sounded that way to him.

He sat back hard in his booth. What was happening to him? He knew he wasn't still dreaming. He was wide awake—the coffee even burned his tongue. Everything was normal, except for those voices.

Abandoning his plate, he rushed out of the diner and headed back to his car. A woman with a long red braid was standing near it, waiting to cross the street. His hands trembled as he sorted through his key chain for the key to open his car door.

"I am my past," the woman said.

He turned around. Once again, he realized she hadn't spoken the words aloud.

"I'll always be what he turned me into. I'll never escape it."

He stood there for a moment, stunned, listening to the voice that seemed to come from nowhere. He saw tears glistening in her eyes as she watched the cars whiz by, and he knew that what he'd heard was something inside her—deep down.

Was he losing his mind?

"*Abuse* is such a clean, sterile word," she went on, and he realized that the preoccupation she seemed to have with waiting for a break in the traffic was really the despair she thought no one could hear.

She glanced his way, and he thought of approaching her, saying something like, *Your past hasn't set your future. There's Jesus Christ. He can change everything.*

But instead, he panicked and got into his car. What if he botched it up? What if she looked at him as one of those Bible-thumping fanatics who went around shoving their beliefs down people's throats? What if he made himself look stupid? Or worse, crazy?

Finally, she crossed the street, hurrying between cars, no longer waiting for a break in the traffic. He heard tires screech and a cab driver cursing, but the woman vanished into the crowd on the sidewalk. Sam sat frozen behind the wheel, marveling at her lack of regard for life . . . or death. The next time she crossed the street, would her desperation plunge her into even greater danger? Would her death wish be granted?

And how had he heard her desperate thoughts?

He sat, paralyzed, behind the wheel. His head was beginning to ache, and tears filled his eyes. His hands were trembling too badly to get the key into the ignition.

He looked at the clock. It was time for him to head for work. If he could just get behind his desk and bury himself in business, he could forget this bizarre morning.

Finally managing to start the car, he pulled out into the traffic and drove the three blocks over to his office building. He turned into the parking garage and found his own space with the sign that read "Sam Bennett, VP, Simpson Advertising." He got out and breathed in the crisp morning air, hoping it would cleanse his brain of this insanity and enable him to function.

He got onto the elevator and spoke to Jimmy, a young man with Down's Syndrome who ran the elevator nine hours a day. "Hi, Jimmy," he said.

"Hi, Mitter Bennett. How are you today?"

He looked down at the floor, waiting for Jimmy to push

the button. "Fine. Just fine." As they rose to the thirteenth floor, he heard Jimmy's voice again.

"Wish I's a real person."

He looked up and saw that Jimmy was sitting on the stool, staring at the numbers as they changed. Sam's heart ached at the simple words he had heard. "Jimmy?" he asked.

"Yes sir, Mitter Bennett," the young man said.

"You are a real person."

"Yes sir, Mitter Bennett."

Confused, and not certain now whether he'd really heard Jimmy or not, Sam stumbled out when the doors opened. Behind him, Jimmy called, "Have a good day, Mitter Bennett."

Sam nodded and gave him a cursory wave, then headed for his office. He passed his secretary on the way in.

"Mornin', Sam," she said. "How's it going?"

"Good, Sally. Any messages so far?"

"Not yet."

He stood at her desk and scanned her calendar to see what was on his agenda today. She pulled her chair up and began jotting his appointments on a separate sheet of paper.

"Eleven, six, fifty-seven."

He glanced at her and saw that she was busy writing. "What was that?" he asked.

She looked up at him, perplexed. "What?"

"Didn't you say something?" He was sweating now. His tie felt too tight; it was constricting his breath.

"I said no messages."

"No! After that."

Slowly, she got up. "Sam, are you sure you're all right? You're looking a little pale."

"I'm fine," he snapped. "Maybe I need a glass of water."

"I'll get you one."

As she headed quickly for the lounge, Sam went into his office and sat down. Things were getting too weird. Nothing made any sense. Sally brought him the water, and he gulped it down, but it didn't do much to help him.

"Do you have a fever?" she asked, touching his forehead maternally.

"No, I just didn't sleep very well last night. I keep thinking I'm hearing people talking." He frowned, realizing what she must be thinking. He was delusional. But he didn't hear any such thought from her. Instead, she repeated, "Eleven, six, fifty-seven . . . It has to win. It has to."

Sam sucked in a breath. "A lottery ticket?" he asked.

The question startled her. She looked as though she'd just gotten caught stealing. "I didn't—"

"No, don't defend yourself," he said, getting up. "I don't care. I just want to know. Are you trying to win the lottery?"

She looked embarrassed for a moment, then after a few seconds, compressed her lips and threw her chin up. "Yes, Sam, I am. You see, I don't make the kind of money you make, so I have to take other opportunities."

"The numbers," he said. "Were they eleven, six, fifty-seven?"

Her gasp could have sucked in an insect from the other side of town. "I knew it!" she shouted. "They're winning numbers. First I heard them on the radio. This guy had kids ages eleven and six, and it was fifty-seven degrees when I got up. And those are the numbers of my birthday! And there were eleven red lights on the way to work and six stop signs, and I saw a flock of birds that must have had fifty-seven—"

He moaned and dropped back down. "Sally, this is a stretch. You're looking for those numbers, but the chances of your winning—"

"Then how come you just spouted them out to me? It's affirmation, Sam! If I wasn't sure before, I am now! The Lord gave me these numbers!"

"Sally, the Lord does a lot of things, but I don't think he picks lottery numbers. My understanding is that he isn't big on gambling."

"Well, you just wait and see," she said.

"If I win, he'll see what I'm worth." This time her lips didn't move.

There it was again. One of those thoughts. He wiped the sweat from his forehead and covered his ears.

"You don't look so good, Sam," she said. "Maybe I should call Kate. She could get you in to see a doctor."

"I don't need a doctor. It's these stupid voices!"

"I had a friend once who kept hearing voices, and it turned out she was picking up radio waves on her fillings. You don't have any new fillings, do you?"

"It's not the radio. It's . . . real voices." He was making no sense at all. This was madness. These voices obviously weren't real, or he would see the mouths move. Maybe he was still dreaming. Maybe he just needed to wake up.

But it didn't feel like a dream.

He got to his feet. "You know, come to think of it, maybe I do need a doctor." He ran his shaking hands through his hair. "Uh . . . look, cover for me for a couple of hours, will you? I need to get out of here, get some fresh air."

"Sure thing, Sam. Your first appointment isn't until eleven, so don't worry about it."

He practically ran up the hall to get away, but he changed his mind before he got to the elevator. He didn't want to be on it with Jimmy again, so he took the stairwell and ran all thirteen floors down. He was perspiring and out of breath when he got to his car. He just needed some Tylenol, he thought. He needed to go to the closest store and get some medicine to help him.

There was a supermarket a mile up the street, so he drove there as fast as he could, almost running over a pedestrian as he turned into the parking lot. He pulled into handicap parking and sat there for a moment, feeling as disabled as anyone who couldn't walk. Finally, he got out and headed in.

He had never been to this store before, so he didn't know where the Tylenol would be. He headed up aisle one and passed a woman standing with a jar of peanut butter in her hand. "We're gonna go hungry," he heard her say. "I can't provide."

He turned around and knew instantly she hadn't said it aloud. She gave him a startled glance and put the peanut butter back. He shrugged out of his coat and almost ran into a teenaged couple standing in front of the school supplies. They were discussing the size of index cards they needed, but as he passed, he heard two other simultaneous voices.

"The pressure . . . it's too much."

"I just want somebody to love me."

He bolted around the corner, and thankfully, came to the Tylenol. He grabbed at the first package he saw, knocking the rest off of the shelf. Trembling, he knelt down and began picking up the boxes. A woman who worked there came up and started helping him. "Are you all right, sir?"

"Yes . . . fine . . . just a little clumsy . . ." He got to his feet and tried to stack the boxes again.

"I'm nobody. He won't even look me in the eye," a voice said.

He told himself he wasn't hearing what he was hearing and took off up the aisle to the cash register. Standing there, his heart pounding, he waited for the man in front of him to pay.

"I miss my family. What have I done?" The man's mouth was set in a grim line as he sorted through his wallet.

Sam turned away and saw the woman with the peanut butter behind him. "They'll go to bed hungry again. I can't take care of myself, much less them."

He tried to open the Tylenol package, but his hand was shaking too badly. He heard the girl behind the cash register muttering, "This is as good as it gets."

Deciding that the Tylenol wasn't going to help anyway, he dropped it onto the belt, pushed past the man, and ran back out to his car.

He got in and locked the door and sat there for a moment, revel-ing in the silence. He didn't want to get out again. He couldn't take the chance of being around people, of hearing those voices.

He needed help, he thought. Someone to talk to. Some-one to tell him what was happening to him. He thought of John, his pastor. John had always listened to him, even before Sam gave his life to Christ. He was a good listener. Nothing had shocked John, not even Sam's sinful past.

He pulled out of the parking lot, and driving as if his mental health depended on his speed, he headed for the church.

3

J OHN WAS JUST PULLING INTO THE CHURCH PARKING lot when Sam drove up. It seemed late—midmorning at least. But as the pastor waved and got out of his car, Sam realized that it was not quite eight. None of the rest of the church staff had made it in yet.

He got out and leaned wearily against the hood as John came around his car. "Sam, are you all right?"

"No," he said. "No, I'm not. Can I talk to you in private?"

John looked around as if to say that they *were* in private, then said, "Sure. Let's go into my office."

Sam managed to hold his confusion in as John escorted him into the church and up the hall to his office. He hadn't been in John's office in a very long time, not since he'd helped paint the place three years before. He went in and slumped down in the chair across from John's desk.

John took the chair next to him and sat facing him. His elbows on his knees, he leaned forward in a gesture of concern. "Tell me, Sam. What's wrong?"

"I can hear things," Sam blurted. "Everywhere I go . . . I hear voices. Talking at me from every direction, every person I pass. I think I'm losing it!"

John sat straighter, letting the words sink in. "What kind of voices?"

Sam got up and went to the window, looked out, and raked his hand through his hair. "Just . . . voices. Like thoughts."

"Talking to you?"

"No, not me, really. It's like . . . it really doesn't have anything to do with me. I just overhear. Like I'm eavesdropping . . ."

He swung back around and saw the twisted expression on the pastor's face. He sounded like someone on drugs, Sam realized.

"Sam, how long have you been this way?"

"Since I woke up." He remembered the dream, and his eyebrows arched. He hurried back to his chair. "I had this dream last night. It was so vivid, John. About some woman looking all over her house for money."

"Money? Sam, are you having financial problems?"

"No! It wasn't about money. It was just a quarter or something. She found it and started celebrating like it was really important. It didn't make any sense. But I'm standing there, part of it, and not part of it . . . wondering what the big deal is with one lost coin."

John sat back in his chair and nodded as if he'd heard all this before. "Sam, did you fall asleep reading the Bible yesterday, by any chance? Had you been reading from Luke 15?"

Sam shook his head. "Luke 15? No. Why?"

"Because I mentioned it in my sermon yesterday. Remember?"

Sam wished he had paid more attention. "No . . . refresh my memory."

John didn't look surprised. "In Luke 15 Jesus tells about a lost coin and a lost sheep and a lost son. It sounds like you were just dreaming about that, maybe processing my sermon."

Sam looked down at his feet. He didn't think it had come out of the Bible—he hadn't read from Luke in a long time. Then he thought about the foreign word that had shaken him so and looked quickly up. "I woke up, and I know I was awake . . . and there was this voice . . . It had all this power and authority, like it was God, himself . . . and he said something in another language."

John's brow furrowed as if he was trying to follow every word. "What did he say?"

"*Ephphatha,* I think. Something like that. You know what that means?"

"No." John thought for a moment. "So that's the voice you heard? That's why you think you're going crazy?"

"No, not just that." Sam got up again and walked across the room, combing his fingers through his sweat-dampened hair. "I was at the diner where I eat breakfast every day, and I heard the waitress—her thoughts or something. I looked up, and she hadn't said anything. And the lady next to me . . . she said gravity was going to let her go, and she was going to fly out in the universe and nobody would notice. I looked at her, and, John, she hadn't said anything. She was just staring down at her coffee. And then the man at the table, and the woman crossing the street, and the elevator guy, and my secretary . . ."

"You heard all of their thoughts?"

"Not their thoughts. I couldn't read their thoughts. Just . . . their feelings, I guess. I don't know." He sat back down. "John, you've got to help me. I don't know what to do."

John took in a deep breath, and looking troubled, he got up and went around his desk. "Sam, I'm gonna refer you to a counselor. You need to talk to a professional."

"Like . . . a shrink?" Sam asked. He remembered telling his wife she needed psychiatric help. He had been kidding, but John was not. The idea didn't thrill him, but he would do anything to get to the bottom of this. A shrink probably saw things like this all the time. Maybe there was some logical explanation. Food poisoning or a bump on the head he'd forgotten about. Maybe he could stop the voices. "That's okay," he said as his mind reeled with possibilities. "That's good. Maybe he can help me."

John flipped through his Rolodex for the name, pulled

out a card, and wrote the number. Sam knew he didn't believe him about the voices, but it didn't much matter, as long as he got some help.

"I don't belong in ministry. Nobody listens. I'm not making an impact."

Sam looked up. "Sure, you do."

John stopped writing. "What?"

"You make an impact. You definitely make an impact. You're not thinking of leaving the ministry just because of wackos like me . . . ?"

John's face changed radically, and he sat frozen, staring back at Sam.

Then Sam realized what he had done. "You didn't say anything, did you? You thought it or felt it. I heard it, John. Don't you see?"

John looked as startled as Sam. "I hadn't told anybody that," he said. "I hadn't discussed this even with my wife. It's just been going through my mind . . ."

"I heard it, John! I'm not making this up! Now can you see what I'm going through?"

John was beginning to perspire now. He rubbed his chin for a moment, staring at Sam with stricken eyes. Slowly, he got up, came back around the desk, and sat in the chair opposite Sam. "Sam, can you hear what I'm thinking right now?"

Sam closed his eyes and tried to listen. It was useless. He couldn't hear on demand. He had no power over what was happening to him. "No. I'm not psychic. It's not like that. It's more like I hear . . . needs. Specific ones."

"Needs? Could you hear people's orders in the diner? Before they spoke?"

"No, not those kinds of needs. It's like . . . what you said in church Sunday, about what would happen if we could hear people's spiritual needs."

John sat back in his chair, silent for a moment. "I didn't think you were listening."

"I wasn't," Sam admitted. "It just sort of came back to me this morning. After God spoke that word."

"You really feel it was God who said that to you?"

Again, he struggled to think it through logically but came back to the same conclusion. "Yes, I do think it was God. I mean, think about it. I'm dreaming about Luke 15, I hear a word in some other language, I remember part of your sermon . . . That stuff never happens to me."

"Thanks a lot," John said.

"But I start hearing all these things . . ."

John went to his bookshelf and got down his concordance. "What was the word again?"

"*Ephphtha* or something."

"*Epithet?*"

"No. It wasn't English. I'm sure it wasn't."

"*Ephah?* That's a measurement."

"No. It had another syllable, I think. Let me see." Sam

took the book and scanned the *Eph's,* whispering the pronunciation of each word. *"Epher, Ephesus, Ephod . . ."* His eyes widened as he came to the word. *"Ephphatha!* This is it! John, this is the word."

John took the book and found the reference. "It's Mark 7:34." He grabbed up his Bible, scanned the verses, then dropped back into his chair. "Wow."

"What?" Sam took the Bible and found the verse. Slowly, he began to read. "He looked up to heaven and with a deep sigh said to him, *'Ephphatha!'* (which means, 'Be opened!')." Sam frowned up at the pastor. "So what was God trying to say to me?"

"Look at the context," John said. "They had brought Jesus a deaf, mute man. And Jesus spat on his fingers and put them into his ears and said, *'Ephphatha!* Be opened.' And the man began to hear and speak."

"But what has that got to do with me? I'm not even hard of hearing."

John got that look in his eyes that he got when he thought the Holy Spirit was moving in their church services. He was obviously getting excited. "Don't you see, Sam? For some reason, the Lord came to you last night, and he opened your ears. Is it possible, Sam, that you're hearing what the Holy Spirit hears? Out loud?"

Sam sorted back through the things he'd heard and slowly began to nod. "I heard a woman who couldn't provide for her family, another woman who thought she'd never escape her past, somebody who thought she was nobody, insignificant . . ."

"Spiritual needs. Just as God hears them."

Sam thought about it for a moment. "Yes, I guess so. But . . . why me? Why would God choose me to curse?"

"Sam, this isn't a curse! This is a gift!" John said. "What I wouldn't give to have it!"

"But why me? Why not somebody like you who knows how to explain about Jesus? Somebody who's comfortable with sharing their faith?"

"We're all supposed to witness whether we're comfortable or not, Sam. That's what I preached on Sunday. We're all supposed to go out there with the feeling of urgency because there are lost people and no one to find them!"

"*But I can't do that!*" Sam shouted. "I'm just an ordinary guy! I'm not a preacher. I've never been to seminary. What am I supposed to do? Preach on the street corners? Go around proclaiming Jesus from the mountaintops?"

"Yes!" John said, springing to his feet.

Sam let out a disbelieving breath and wilted back into the chair. "John, you've got to help me. I can't do this."

"Sure you can," John said, leaning toward him and taking his shoulder. "Sam, if you're a Christian you can do this. You've been given a mighty gift, and the Lord never gives a gift he doesn't equip you to use."

"But this is insane. Kate'll have me committed."

"Not if she hears her deepest spiritual needs spoken back to her like you just did with me. People will listen to you, Sam! They want nothing more than to find the answers to their deepest needs—they'll *want* you to talk to them! Do you know how special that is?"

Sam felt suddenly overwhelmed. He dropped his face into his hands and began to cry, something he hadn't done since his mother's funeral years ago. This was too much for one man to handle.

John laid his hand on the back of Sam's neck. "Sam, I want to pray for you. This seems like a lot, I know. But God gave it to you. You need to thank him and acknowledge that you can't use it without him. It's *his* power."

Sam could accept that; this wasn't something of his own doing. Only God could have come up with something this amazing. He bowed his head, still crying, and listened as John prayed for him. He wished he could believe that the Lord would just fill him with words and courage and that Sam could tell everyone he saw how to meet those needs, just like Paul or Peter. But he had trouble seeing himself in that role. Since when was Sam Bennett a missionary evangelist? When John whispered, "Amen," Sam looked helplessly up at him.

"Sam, I'll help you," John said. "How about if we each take the day off? We can go somewhere and sit. You can just tell me everything you hear. I'll take it from there. I'll teach you how to let God direct."

Sam felt the first calm of the day washing over him like a warm tide, and he squinted up at John through his tears. "You could do that?"

"Of course I could. I can't wait to see how this works."

He opened his hands. "All right. Where will we go?"

John thought a moment. "The bus station? It's sometimes pretty crowded this time of day. Think of all those lost souls. All those voices."

"No." Sam shook his head adamantly. "I can't handle that. Just a few at a time. Let's go someplace I'm used to. Let's go back to the diner."

"All right," John said. "Let me just leave a note for the staff."

But as they headed back out to John's car, Sam felt a sinking, sick feeling deep in his gut that God had made his first mistake.

4

SINCE SAM WAS SO DISTRACTED, JOHN DROVE following Sam's directions to the diner. The place was even more crowded than it had been when he'd been here earlier. Sam looked at his watch and realized that it wasn't that late in the day; it was only 9:30 a.m. He'd gotten an awfully early start today. Dozens of people still crammed in to grab breakfast before heading to work.

John followed him in and looked around for a booth. Janie, the waitress, lifted her voice over the noise. "Good thing you came back, Sam, since you ran out of here without paying me this morning."

Sam hadn't thought of it until now. Embarrassed, he made his way to the counter. "I'm sorry, Janie. I wasn't thinking clearly. But you knew I'd be back, didn't you?"

"Sure," Janie said, waving him off. "You've never stiffed me before." She pointed to the booth in the corner. Two orderlies from the hospital were just leaving it. "Why don't you take that one, and I'll get Joe to come out and wipe the table for you. Joe!"

John looked around as if he was a little shell-shocked at the noise and crowd as they took the sticky table. Sam gestured toward Janie as they sat down. "I heard her voice this morning."

"What did it say?" John asked.

"Something about rest. That it could change her whole life. That doesn't sound like a spiritual need to me, does it to you?"

John considered that for a moment. "Jesus said, 'Come to me all ye who are weary and heavy laden, and I will give you rest.'"

Sam rubbed his jaw. "Sure did, didn't he? How about that?"

"So did you tell her that?"

"No, I didn't tell her anything. I didn't know what was happening. It surprised me when I realized she didn't know I'd heard her. And then that lady next to me said that thing about gravity letting her go, and—"

"Is she here now?"

Sam looked around. "No, she's gone."

"So how did you answer her?"

Sam grunted out his annoyance. "I didn't. She got irritated when I tried, so I moved to another table."

"Oh." John was clearly disappointed. "Did you talk to anybody about what you heard?"

"Of course not. They would have called the police or something." He stared across the table at his pastor, wondering what he expected.

"So what are you hearing right now?" John asked.

Sam drew in a deep breath and sat back in his booth, listening.

"I can't do this alone." The voice startled him, and he turned to the table next to theirs and saw a pregnant girl with a toddler.

He turned back to John and tried to cover his mouth. "The woman next to us—she said she can't do this alone."

John's eyes danced like those of a kid at the gates of an amusement park. "Go tell her she doesn't have to."

Sam shifted in his seat. He was sorry he'd ever brought John into this. "I can't do that!"

"Why not?"

"Because. She doesn't know I heard her thoughts. She'll think it's a pickup line."

"No, she won't. If you go up and address her deepest spiritual need, you think she's gonna turn you away?"

"Well, no, but . . . come on, John. I come here every day. I know some of these people. I don't want them to start running from me."

John's expression fell. "He hasn't heard a word I've said."

The words didn't come through his lips, and Sam's face grew hot.

He leaned forward, locking eyes with his pastor. "I have too heard what you've said, John. Stop thinking you're a failure because I'm not Billy Graham."

"God isn't asking you to be Billy Graham," John said. "Sam, why do you think God gave you this ability?"

"I don't know. I've been asking myself that all morning. I guess it's punishment for being lukewarm or something."

"It's not a punishment," John whispered. "It's a wonderful gift. What are you afraid of?"

"I don't know. Of messing somebody's head up. Of telling them the wrong thing. Of turning them off to religion altogether because they think I'm some kind of Bible-waving maniac."

John seemed to look right into him. Sam hated that about him. "It's not really any of those things, is it, Sam?"

"You got the gift too?" Sam demanded. "You think you can look into my heart and see what I'm feeling? Well, why don't you just tell me what it is?"

John kept his eyes locked on Sam's. "I think you're embarrassed. Ashamed."

"Ashamed!" He thought of leaving—just storming out in righteous indignation. "I'm not ashamed of my faith!"

"Then how many times have you told anybody else about it?"

"Plenty!" he said. "They can see by my life. People know that I don't do business the same way they do. I treat others kindly. They know I'm active at church. They *know*, okay?"

"But how many times have you shared it out loud? In words? How many people have you led to Christ?"

"None that I know of, but that doesn't mean I'm ashamed. It just means that the situation hasn't come up." He stopped and stared at his preacher across the table. Even without his gift, Sam knew what John was thinking. He was making excuses. Sam rubbed his face. "Look, John, there's nothing I'd like better than to be able to say I've led a bunch of people to Christ. Every Christian would like to think that. But I'm not like you. That's not my gift. I'm not bold that way. I mean, what if I get over there and start telling that woman about Jesus, and she asks me some theological question that I can't answer, because frankly—and I'll just be honest here—I haven't studied the Bible all that much."

"Do you know Jesus?" John asked.

Sam looked at him, astonished. "Yes, John! Can you really ask me that? You baptized me. I may not be the greatest Christian who ever lived, but I do have a relationship with Christ."

"Then tell her about that," John said. "That's all she needs to know right now. That's all *you* need to know right now."

Sam couldn't believe the pastor was putting him on the

spot this way. Did John think it was that simple? "I don't even know how to start the conversation. I mean, what do I do? Go plop down at her table and tell her that she doesn't have to do this alone? What if she doesn't even realize that was what she was thinking? What if—"

John's eyes were laughing. "You know, Sam, Satan doesn't have to do anything to foil your attempts to get the word out. You're doing his job for him."

Sam leaned back hard in his booth. "Oh, that's low. That's really low, John."

"Why do you think God is letting you hear these voices?"

He clenched his hands into fists. "To drive me crazy."

"No," John said. "He obviously wants you to respond to them. You wouldn't just be hearing these things if you weren't supposed to respond in some way."

"So you're saying that every time I hear these voices I'm supposed to launch into some kind of amateur sermon?"

"Maybe that's the plan."

"I probably heard six voices at one time in the grocery store. Was I supposed to climb up on an egg crate and start preaching to them?"

"You tell me."

"Come on, John!"

John looked over at the woman, and Sam followed his gaze. She was helping the child eat some hash browns while her other hand rubbed the top of her belly. "I'm scared," Sam heard her say, though she hadn't really said it. "I don't want to do this."

He wondered if she was headed to the hospital for an appointment. If there was a husband in her life. If she really was alone or just *felt* alone. Suddenly, he forgot where he and John were in their argument.

John had obviously forgotten too. The pastor slid out of the booth.

Sam caught his arm. "Where are you going?"

"Just right here to talk to this lady," he whispered.

Sam let go and watched John approach her. "Ma'am, I'm John Ingalls, Pastor of Church of the Savior over on Post Road," he said gently, "and I was just noticing this precious little girl."

The young woman smiled. "Thank you."

"Do you mind if I sit down for just a second? I'd like to talk to you if you have a minute."

She shrugged. "Sure, go ahead."

That was it, Sam thought. That was the place where he would have struck out. She would have taken one look at him and yelled for help. He'd often had that effect on women.

But John had that kind, non-threatening face. It was clear from a mile away that the man was a preacher.

Janie brought Sam coffee, and he began meticulously mixing the sugar and cream into it as he listened to the conversation at the next table.

"I noticed the way you kept rubbing your stomach," John said. "I just wondered if you're all right."

She breathed a laugh. "Well, frankly, I may not be."

"What do you mean?"

"I'm kind of in labor."

Sam's head came up.

"Why aren't you in the hospital?" John asked.

"I've been there already," she said. "They told me I'm just in the early stages. That I should come back when the contractions are closer together. They said to walk around a little, relax . . ."

"Well, have you notified your husband?"

She shook her head. "I don't have a husband."

"Well, the baby's father, then. Isn't there—?"

Tears sprang to her eyes, and she put her hand over her mouth. The little girl looked up at her, touched her, as if the tears were familiar, yet still dreadful.

John leaned forward on the table and met her eyes. "You must be feeling pretty alone right now."

Sam's eyes shot across to John. He was using what Sam had told him about her need. She nodded fiercely. "That's exactly how I'm feeling."

"Do you have someone to keep this sweet little girl while you're in the hospital?"

She wiped her eyes. "No. Social Services is going to take her until I get out. I don't see why she can't just stay there with me. She's real good . . ." Her voice trailed off as she put her arm around the tiny child's shoulders.

John was shaking his head. "Look, my wife and I would love to baby-sit for you while you're in the hospital. We love kids, and our baby just went off to college this year. She could stay with us for as long as you want her to."

The prospect seemed to trouble her more. She took the child's hand and laced their fingers together. "Thank you, but I don't know . . ."

"Of course you wouldn't trust me just like that," John said. "Call my church and ask about me. I could get my wife to come here so you could meet her. If you don't feel good about us after all that, then we'll just go our separate ways and leave you alone."

She stared across the table. "Why would you do that? Baby-sit for someone you've never met?"

"Because something told me that you were alone and you needed it. And to be perfectly honest, I needed an opening so I could explain to you that you're not really alone, that there's someone who loved you enough to die for you. And because he loves you so much, he sat me down at the table next to you, so I could come and tell you."

As if he was the one to whom John referred, she looked over at Sam, still alone at the next table. "Someone loved me?" she asked, almost disgusted. "Who?"

"Jesus Christ," he said.

Her face changed, and he saw the cynicism that lined her young face. "Oh, come on. Give me a break."

"No, listen to me," John said, brooking no debate. "You are not alone. You may feel like you are, but there are people out there who can love you and care for you, and the only reason they can is that Jesus does."

She rubbed her stomach. "If only I could believe that."

"You can believe it," he said. "It's true."

The woman's face began to redden, and it twisted as she began to weep. The little girl set down her spoon and stared up at her mother. John touched the woman's shoulder. "Ma'am, this doesn't have to go on, this feeling of solitude. When you bring that baby into the world today, you could bring it into a Christian home."

She looked down at her stomach, then over at the child. "I've never taken her to church," she said. "I've never taught her anything about the Bible. There's so much I would have to learn."

"You don't have to learn anything before you come to Christ," John said. "All you have to do is pray and tell Jesus that you want him to take over your life. Do you want to do that?"

Still weeping, she nodded her head. "It couldn't be any worse than it's been." She breathed in a sob. "Yes, I'd like to do that."

John met Sam's eyes, quietly saying, *See? You could do*

this. But Sam knew better—John was a natural. "Let's pray," John said.

She looked awkwardly around her. "I don't know if I can do this right out in public . . ."

"He died right out in public," John whispered. "Don't let embarrassment keep you from that kind of love."

John closed his eyes, and the woman followed. Sam listened as John began to lead her in prayer, and he felt the thrill of witnessing a new convert being ushered into the kingdom of God. He couldn't believe it had been so easy. He'd heard stories of doors being slammed in people's faces, persecutions, even. He'd read about that in the Bible.

Then the thought came to him. *I've made it easy for you, Sam.*

He drew in a deep breath as they came out of the prayer, and the tension on the woman's face began to drain away as she laughed through her tears. She was not much more than a teenager, he realized. Practically a kid. About his daughter's age. His heart jolted at the thought of Jennifer, a college freshman, in labor with no one beside her. How could that have happened to this young woman?

John kept talking to her, and after a moment, he got up and went to the pay phone. Sam knew he was calling his wife to come and get the little girl. He wondered how often John put Christ's love into such concrete action. Maybe that was what they were all supposed to do, he thought. Maybe

Christians, like doctors, were supposed to heal fatal spiritual ills, terminal diseases of the soul.

When John came back, he put Sam on the spot. "Sam, come here for a minute. I want you to meet the newest member of our family."

Sam got awkwardly up and reached for her hand.

"You're brothers?" the woman asked.

"No," Sam said quickly.

"Brothers in Christ," John said. "And now you're our sister."

Her eyes filled again as she laughed softly. "Oh. Right."

Sam sat down at the table. He didn't know what to say.

The child stood up, revealing her wet pants. "Uh-oh," she said. "We haven't quite got this potty training down." She got to her feet, her hand on her stomach. "Would you all excuse me for a minute, please? I'm leaving my bag here."

Sam looked under the table and saw her duffel bag for the hospital. She carried a diaper bag and purse on her shoulder.

"If you'd just keep an eye on it, I'll be right back."

"Sure," John said. "Are you sure you'll be all right?"

"Oh, yeah. I've probably got hours yet. I'll just yell out if anything happens."

They disappeared into the rest room, and John grinned back at Sam. "So what do you think about that?"

"I think that was amazing," Sam said. "The most amazing thing I've ever seen."

"You could do it too. It's very simple. You know their needs. Address them."

But Sam was still skeptical. It was one thing to know their needs. It was another to meet them.

"I'm so dirty." The voice behind him was as loud as if it had been whispered right in his ear, and he turned around and saw the man sitting there, in a clean, pressed suit, reading the newspaper as if nothing was wrong. "I can't stand my life anymore. I'm filthy, tainted."

Sam turned back to John. "The man behind me," he said. "He said he feels dirty, tainted, filthy."

John's serious eyes locked into his. "Go tell him, Sam. Tell him how he can get clean."

Sam closed his eyes. He didn't want to be here. He didn't want this responsibility on him, this accountability. He was getting a headache. He needed to lie down.

"Go on," the pastor urged.

Sam rubbed his temples. "You better do it," he said. "You've had more experience with this sort of thing."

"Sam, just talk to him."

"What do I say?" he whispered harshly. "How do I lead in? 'Excuse me, but I couldn't help overhearing your soul crying out?'"

"No," John said. "Just tell him what happened to you."

Sam sighed as the woman and her child made their way back to the table. John obviously needed to keep talking to her about her newfound faith and the baby on the way. Sam realized he was stuck. If he didn't do it, his pastor would think he was a coward. Slowly, he got up and turned to the chair behind him. "Excuse me," he said.

The man looked up from the newspaper. "Yeah?"

"I'm sorry to bother you," Sam said. "I'm just . . . well, you see, I kind of have this gift, and I can sort of . . . hear things . . ."

The man's eyes narrowed. He wasn't following what Sam was saying. Sam put his hand on the chair and started to pull it out. "May I?"

The man leaned suspiciously back in his chair. "Sure, go ahead."

"Well, you see, I couldn't help overhearing . . ."

The man was quiet, waiting.

". . . something you may not realize you said." Sam stopped and realized he was taking the wrong route. He didn't need to be quite that direct.

"I'm sorry; I don't understand."

"Of course you don't. Uh . . . look, man." He leaned his elbows on the table and got closer, keeping his voice confidentially low. "This isn't going to make any sense to you, but I felt like I should come over here and tell you something about myself."

The man looked as if he was bracing himself for a sales pitch.

"A few years ago . . . I did some things . . . saw some things . . . put some things into my head that . . . well, they just made me feel really dirty."

The man's face changed. Sam knew he had his attention.

"I don't want to go into the details," Sam said. "But let me just say that I really felt that I couldn't stand my life anymore. I got to the point where I thought that if there was a God, he must be awfully disgusted with me."

The man sat stone still . . . listening.

"And then one night I was sitting at home with my wife, who's this strong Christian woman, and she'd been dragging me to church by the hand for years and years . . . and I just about lost it. I started to cry, and I couldn't stop crying, and I began to confess to her everything I was doing. My wife . . . she got up and got her Bible and opened it to this one section I'd never seen before." He shrugged. "Of course I hadn't seen it. I never listened in church, never paid any attention, never read it. But it said that while we were yet sinners, Christ died for us."

The man looked down at the table. His hands were trembling. Sam was getting to him, he thought. It was working.

"And it really got to me, you see, because there I was telling my wife my darkest secrets, not thinking even she could forgive me, and there she was telling me that somebody died for me, to take my punishment for all the filth, even when I was his enemy."

The man's nostrils flared. He closed his hands into fists over his newspaper and brought his eyes up to Sam's. "Are you finished?"

Sam's heart sank. He'd thought he had him, but now it was clear he'd gone too far. "Well . . . yes. I just wanted to tell you because—"

"Then would you kindly let me eat in peace?" the man bit out.

Sam didn't know what to say. Confused, he scooted his chair back. "Yeah, sure. Okay. But . . . if you ever want to talk or anything . . ."

"To you?" the man asked with disdain. He almost laughed. "Thanks, pal. But if I ever needed to talk, it wouldn't be to some born-again sleazeball who peddles his religion like cheap watches. I have a life." With that, he folded his newspaper and got up.

Sam dug into his pocket for his business card. "Look, just take this, in case you ever—"

"Didn't you hear me, pal? I don't need what you're selling."

"Yes, you do."

The man laughed then. Shaking his head, he tossed down some money for his meal, and bolted out the door.

Sam felt as if the wind had been knocked out of him. He stayed at the table, running the conversation back through his mind, trying to figure out where he had gone wrong.

Later, when John's wife had come and taken the little girl

home and her mother had gone for a walk to speed up her contractions, Sam and John left the diner. "I guess I failed pretty miserably in there, didn't I?" Sam asked.

John gave him an amused look across the hood of the car. "You've got to be kidding. You were great."

"Great? That guy practically ran out. It couldn't have gone worse."

"But that's not your fault. The Lord revealed the man's need to you, and you were obedient and responded. If he rejected it, he's accountable to God, not you."

"How do you know that?"

Before Sam knew what was happening, John had whipped a small Bible out of his shirt pocket and was turning to Ezekiel. "Says so right here. Chapter 3 of Ezekiel." He slid the Bible across the seat. "Read for yourself. Verses 18 and 19."

Sam took the Bible and began to mumble the words. "When I say to a wicked man, 'You will surely die,' and you do not warn him or speak out to dissuade him from his evil ways in order to save his life, that wicked man will die for his sin, and I will hold you accountable for his blood."

Sam stopped on the last word, suddenly remembering the woman with the red braid this morning, walking through traffic with no regard for her life. He hadn't told her what he knew. If she'd been hit by that skidding car and died without knowing Christ, he would have been accountable.

He felt the blood drain from his face.

"Read on," John said. "Just the next verse."

"But if you do warn the wicked man and he does not turn from his wickedness or from his evil ways . . ."

"Like the guy who just rejected you," John interjected.

". . . he will die for his sin; but you will have saved yourself."

"You won't be accountable," John said, "because you warned him."

"Well, that's fine for me," Sam said. "But what about him? Why wouldn't he listen if I addressed his real spiritual need?"

"Some won't ever listen," John said. "There will always be those who reject the truth. That can't stop us."

Sam closed his eyes and leaned his head against the window. "I still feel like a failure. If I'd gone about it another way . . . approached him differently. . . What good is this gift?"

"It did the woman good," John said. "I wouldn't have known what she needed if you hadn't told me."

"Still . . . you were right about me, John. I'm pitiful. I've been a Christian for ten years, and not once in those ten years have I ever led anybody to Christ. Until about an hour ago, I never even wanted to."

"Well, don't look now, but I think things are about to change. With this gift, God is leading you straight to the front lines."

Sam was silent for several moments. "I don't know if I'm ready for this, John."

"Sam, God doesn't wait for you to be ready. Sometimes he just throws you in. It's not a real hard thing, talking about Jesus. You don't have to take a class; you don't have to read a book; you don't have to memorize an outline. All you really have to do is tell them what he did for you. That's the best testimony there is."

Sam nodded his head slowly and wished that he had the confidence and passion that John had. Instead, he had a sick feeling that he was going to let the Lord down. The angels in heaven were probably bracing themselves in dread at all the damage he was about to do.

5

A FTER MUCH PERSUADING, JOHN CONVINCED SAM to join him on his hospital visits. As they walked across the street, Sam began to feel uneasy again. "You know, I'm not very good with sick people. I hope you plan to do all the talking. I think I almost gave that guy at the diner a heart attack. His face was beet red when I got through with him."

John didn't seem worried. In fact, Sam could almost see the wheels turning in his head. "One of my greatest frustrations as a pastor is when members of my flock are about to die and I can't look into their spirit and tell for sure if they know the Lord. That's why I want you to come. I think it would help me a lot if you could just tell me what you hear when you sit in their room, so I'll know which way to lead the conversation and how to address their needs."

"But I can't just repeat back to you what I hear," Sam said. "They'd get wise."

"Wise to what?" John asked. "Wise to the fact that someone knew their spiritual needs? That last guy is proof that they're not even thinking these things consciously. You could probably repeat them right back to them verbatim, and they may not even recognize them."

"You recognized them when I repeated your needs."

"But I'm already a Christian. I've prayed about what you heard. I've looked my problems in the face."

Sam couldn't help remembering the needs he'd heard in John. "You aren't really thinking about leaving the ministry, are you?"

Several moments passed before John answered. "Yeah, actually, I am."

"Why? I thought you loved preaching."

"I love serving the Lord. But if I'm not making an impact, then I need to get out of it. It's a frustrating profession sometimes, Sam. You stand up in that pulpit, pouring out your heart and soul, and half the congregation just stares back at you with glassy eyes, trying to stifle their yawns. Five minutes after the sermon they can't remember what your main point was. Churches are supposed to grow. Christians are supposed to bear fruit. If neither of those things is happening in my church, then I'm failing."

Sam gaped at him. "I don't get it. You're not failing—how do you figure that? Our church is vibrant. It's great."

John breathed a cynical laugh. "Yeah, we did win the city-wide basketball championship this year, and our softball team is shaping up to be a winner. But that's not what I'm going for.

It's all those pesky lost souls that are troubling me. And all those yawning Christians who don't care about them."

"Oh, come on," Sam said. "I care. But this stuff is hard. I mean, you just said that lots of people don't even know their deepest spiritual needs. If they don't, what's the point? I mean, what can you really do? Even this so-called gift I have, how does it help if they don't recognize their needs when I mention them?"

"The point is that their soul would recognize them. Something inside them would stir, whether they admit it or not. These people we're going to visit in the hospital . . . some of them are scared. They need to know what Jesus can do to help them."

"But don't they have enough problems, being sick and all?"

John shot him a look. "Some of them are going to die. This may be their last chance. That's part of the reason why I insist on visiting members of my church. I don't want anybody to die without understanding completely."

Sam got quiet, thoughtful, as they walked the rest of the way to the hospital. His wife worked here as a nurse, and as they went in, he was assaulted with the mingling smells of sterility and disease. He knew other people couldn't smell it, but it always seemed to jump out at him. That was why he avoided hospitals like the plague. His mother had died in a room on the fourth floor, and he hadn't been back

since. Whenever he picked up Kate, she met him in the parking lot.

He wondered what his wife would say about his being
here now, or about this bizarre gift he'd been cursed with. This
morning, when they'd had coffee together, he hadn't known
about it. Why hadn't he heard her needs? His mind ran back
through their conversation.

I just want to be useful.

The words scampered through his mind. He'd heard her
say that, but now that he thought about it, he hadn't been
looking at her. Had she really said it, or had she felt it?

John glanced over at him as they reached the elevator.
"You okay?"

"Yeah," Sam said. "I'm fine. I was just wondering if I
should tell Kate."

"Why keep it secret from her?"

"I don't know. She might feel violated, knowing I can hear
right into her."

John grinned. "Are you kidding? That's every woman's
dream. To know that her life partner can hear her deepest
needs. The problem will be convincing her, but if you do what
you did with me this morning, she'll believe you."

The elevator doors opened, and John stepped on. Sam was
beginning to get that sick feeling again. "Who are we visiting?"

"Annabelle York."

"Do I know her?"

"She's old. She's been homebound for a while, but until a few months ago she sat in the front row and said 'Amen' to everything I said."

"Oh, yeah. The little white-haired lady. She has been out for a while, hasn't she?" He was ashamed that he hadn't thought of her until now.

"She's got cancer of the liver. They've done everything they can do."

"Well, you're not worried about her spiritual condition, are you? I mean, she's obviously a Christian."

"Maybe, but you can't ever tell. You know what the Bible says. Not everyone who calls 'Lord, Lord,' will enter the kingdom of heaven."

The doors opened, but Sam made no move to get off. "Why would she come to church every Sunday, sit in the front row, shout out 'Amen,' if she wasn't really a Christian?"

"I'm not saying that's the case," John said, catching the elevator door before it could shut. "If I were the judge, I'd say this woman's got it lock, stock, and barrel. But the problem is, a lot of times they fool you. A lot of times they fool themselves. I just don't like taking chances when someone's about to leave the world. I want you to tell me what you hear."

They got off the elevator, and Sam began to feel the dread he'd always felt when he'd approached his mother's room. He looked for an exit door as they walked. "John, how am I gonna do this? I can't just tell you what I hear in front of her."

"Find some way to pose it. I don't care how you do it. Just do it. I need to know."

Once again, Sam resented this gift that he hadn't asked for and didn't want. He slowed as they approached the door to her room. John knocked, and when he didn't hear an answer, pushed the door open, and stuck his head in. "Miss Annabelle, how are you doing, sweetheart?"

Sam grudgingly followed him in. This was rude, he thought, shoving his way into somebody's hospital room when they weren't feeling well. But it was too late to stop the pastor. John was at the bed, leaning over it. The old woman smiled and reached up to take his hand. He squeezed it and asked her softly how she was doing. The woman could barely speak.

"You remember Sam from church, don't you, Miss Annabelle? He's making the rounds with me today."

She smiled weakly and nodded her head, as if she knew him well, but Sam wasn't sure he'd ever been close enough to look her in the eye. "How are you, ma'am?"

"Fine," she mouthed, as if too weak to project. Then he heard a strong voice that wasn't coming from her lips. "It's too late. Way too late. So many years wasted."

Sam took a step back and tried to signal John with his eyes that he'd heard something. Then he realized that if he leaned over and whispered to John, she probably didn't even have the strength to notice.

John's eyes riveted into Sam's, and he nodded for him to pass it on.

"She thinks it's too late," Sam said quietly, and he saw her looking at him, straining to hear. "She thinks she's wasted years."

John frowned as if he didn't know what to make of that. "But does she know the Lord?" John whispered.

As if in answer, the voice came again. "All the people I could have taken to heaven with me. But I was more concerned about doing that busy church work and keeping a clean house."

Yes, Sam thought. She knew Christ. At once, a boldness overtook him and he wanted to talk to her, to help her. He didn't want to play games by whispering to John. He stepped around the bed and got closer to her. "Miss Annabelle," he said. "The Lord has revealed something about you to me. Do you mind if I tell you what it is?"

She shook her head.

"The Lord told me that you're concerned because you didn't lead more people to Christ. That you feel you were more preoccupied with church work and housework than with soul winning."

Her eyes brimmed with tears, and her mouth came open as she tried to speak. She looked from Sam to the preacher and squeezed his hand. "Think . . . how many people . . . I could have helped."

John bent down over her, still holding her gnarled hand. "Miss Annabelle, let me pray for you."

Sam bowed his head as John began to pray for the old woman who was suffering her last hours of life on earth and worrying about coming face to face with the One who knew her original potential.

Later, when they were back out in the hall, John smiled softly. "Miss Annabelle will be in heaven soon."

"Yes, she will," Sam said. "She's definitely a Christian. But she seemed so sad about what she hadn't done."

"I think a lot of us are going to feel that way when we get to the end," John said. "I see that a lot."

They went on to the next room that John had on his list. "Who are we gonna see now?" Sam asked.

"Sid Beautral. You know, Hattie Beautral's husband?"

Sam frowned. "I thought she was a widow."

"No, she just comes alone. He's not big on church. He had gallbladder surgery."

"So he's not dying?"

"No, just recovering."

"Thank goodness," Sam said. They paused at the door and John knocked. A woman called, "Come in."

John pushed the door open. "Hello, Miss Hattie. How are you, Sid?"

John hugged the woman easily, then shook the hand of the man in bed. It seemed second nature to John to embrace the weak, while Sam found creative ways to avoid them.

"What brings you here, Preacher?" the man asked gruffly. "You know I ain't dying."

"Of course you're not," John said. "I don't just visit dying people. I visit anybody in my flock who's in the hospital."

"You count me in your flock?" he asked skeptically.

"Yes, believe it or not, I do. Now, how are you doing?"

Sid shrugged. "Guess I'm okay."

Then Sam heard his voice again, but Sid's lips didn't move. "I'm powerless. Can't defend myself. All my life is in somebody else's control."

Sam nudged John. John nodded, encouraging him to speak. Sam cleared his throat and tapped his hand nervously on the bedrail. "Uh . . . Mr. Beautral, you're probably feeling pretty powerless lying here, like you're not in control . . . like you can't defend yourself."

"Defend myself from what?" the man asked, his eyes narrowing.

Sam was at a loss. "From anything. I don't know. What threatens you?"

The man looked as if he thought Sam was crazy. "Nothing threatens me. I mean, nothing I can think of."

Fortunately, John took it from there, and Sam let out a heavy breath and stepped back. "Sid, you know you don't have to feel powerless," John said. "There is someone in control, and it's someone who loves you and knows the number of hairs on your head."

Miss Hattie smiled, and the man looked up at him, his face changing as his eyes locked into John's. Sam prayed that John would lead this man to Christ before they left here today.

When they got back into the car to leave the hospital, John's eyes were dancing. "I think this has got to be one of the best days of my Christian life."

Sam wished he felt so exuberant, but every muscle in his body was as rigid as stone. He knew the tension would take hours to subside. "I think it's probably one of the worst days of my Christian life," he admitted.

"Why?" John asked. "Don't you feel good knowing that you'll never get to the point where Miss Annabelle is, getting to the end of your life and feeling regret because you never led anyone to Christ? Look at how many people we've influenced just this morning."

"*You've* influenced," Sam said. "I haven't really done anything except repeat back what I've heard."

"You've done more than you know. You've listened, Sam. Not everybody listens."

"Not everybody has to hear what I hear," Sam muttered. "What am I gonna do with this now? How am I gonna get used to this?"

"Maybe you won't ever. Maybe you'll be known as the guy who can nail people's souls. There are worse things people could say about you."

"I don't want that reputation. Or that gift, or whatever you call it. I'm not ready for this."

"Of course you are. If I were to leave you right now at the bus station and you went in there and all those people were standing around, you'd know just what to do."

"No, I wouldn't," he said. "It would freak me out. This morning in the grocery store when I was hearing all those voices at the same time all around me, I thought I was losing my mind."

"Well, if it was possible for you to transfer the gift to me, I'd take it before you could say *Ephphatha.*"

Sam was exhausted by the time John agreed to return to the church. As John went in, Sam got into his car and sat there a moment, thinking. He knew he couldn't handle going to the office, so he called Sally on his cell phone and told her he would be out the rest of the day.

"I bought the lottery ticket, Sam," she said. "Maybe you ought to start looking for another secretary."

He closed his eyes and dropped his head to the steering wheel. "How about I wait until you've gotten the check?"

"All right," she said. "But I can't promise two weeks' notice."

He clicked off the cell phone and thought of the need

he'd heard in her that morning. "*Eleven, six, fifty-seven . . . It has to win. It has to!*"

What if it did? He had heard it out loud, without her uttering the words. It didn't fit the category of "spiritual need" like all the other things he'd heard today. Maybe she was onto something.

He withdrew a pad of paper from his glove compartment and jotted down the numbers—11, 6, 57. He wondered if it was too late to buy a ticket.

He started the car and headed to the closest convenience store that sold lottery tickets, pulled into the parking lot, and idled there for a moment. Then he remembered the rest of what her soul had said.

"*If I win, he'll see what I'm worth.*"

Was that why he'd heard the numbers? Because they were part of her spiritual need?

Could winning the lottery really be someone's spiritual need? Or was it just God's way of giving him an insider's tip?

Eleven, six, fifty-seven.

What was the jackpot this week? How would Sally feel about having to split it with him? Would she feel betrayed, or amazed? And what would his wife think? Would she accept the money when she was so opposed to the lottery, or would she understand that this new gift gave him vital information that he might as well use? Besides, being wealthy could give him more time to help others.

Suddenly, his runaway thoughts screeched to a halt. What he'd heard had been vital information, all right, but he knew deep down that it was not so he could win the lottery. It was so he could win souls to Christ.

He must be crazy. Either that, or Satan was trying to get in on the act. He closed his eyes and asked God for forgiveness.

Maybe hunger and fatigue, when added to his stress, had been the lethal combination that had driven him to such foolishness. He didn't need a lottery ticket anymore than Sally did. He needed food. Two visits to the diner, and he still hadn't eaten. He and John had been too busy going from one place to another, like Paul and Silas, full of the good news and not enough time to tell everyone about it.

We cannot help speaking about what we have seen and heard. It was a quote he had seen when his Sunday school class studied Acts, and it had jumped out at him then. He'd been convicted that there was something wrong with Christians who *could* stop speaking about what they had seen and heard.

But he was one of them. He'd felt bad about that for half a day, and then he'd gotten over it.

Was this how the Lord was disciplining him? God had struck Paul blind to bring him around. Maybe Sam didn't have so much to complain about.

He started the car and decided to head back to the diner for the third time that day. Janie, the waitress, was still behind the counter, accommodating all her customers with the economy of motion of a seasoned waitress. Sam quietly took a table in the corner, away from anyone he could hear, and watched Janie as she waited on the last of the customers. He remembered what she'd said this morning about needing rest—or what her *soul* had said—and realized that something wasn't right in her life. She had a need.

When she'd finally finished with all those customers, she came back to his table. "Sam, I'm starting to think you have a crush on me. Coming in here three times in one day? Aren't you married?"

Sam chuckled. "Yep, I am. It's been a weird day, Janie."

"Aren't you working today?"

"I guess I'm taking the day off. I'm not feeling my best."

"I'm sorry. You're not contagious, are you? I can't afford to get sick."

He grinned. "If only I were."

She frowned. "Huh?"

"Never mind."

She pulled out her menu pad. "Well, what'll it be this time?"

"A hamburger," he said. "With everything. And how about taking a break and keeping me company while I eat it?"

Her mouth dropped open. "What would your wife say?"

"She would agree that you look like you need a rest. For a few minutes, at least."

Her smile faded, and she looked down at him. He wondered if she realized that was what she needed. "Man, I sure could use a rest. Okay, Sam, I'll be right back."

She came back in moments with his meal and a glass of her own iced tea and sat down across from him, gratefully sighing a breath of relief. "It has been some day in here."

"Tell me about it," he said.

She laughed and looked into her iced tea.

"No, I'm serious. I really want you to tell me about it."

She looked up at him, and in that moment he heard the voice again. "I can't go on like this. Everything's going to fall apart."

"It's just been busy," she said aloud. "My feet are killing me."

His brow knit together in concern. "You don't feel like you can go on, do you?" he asked. "Like everything's just going to fall apart."

She frowned and leaned back in her seat. "How did you know that?"

"Have you ever heard the Bible verse . . . I don't even know for sure where it's found. But it's when Jesus said, 'Come to me all ye who are weary . . . something-or-other . . . and I will give you rest.'"

As he watched her slow reaction, he mentally kicked himself for being so inept with Scripture. Had he really said "something-or-other"? He might as well give it up right now, he thought. He didn't have a chance of leading her to Christ.

"Say that again?" she asked.

He wanted to groan. He couldn't make himself ad-lib again, so he decided to paraphrase. "Jesus said to come to him, and he will give you rest."

"I've heard about that kind of rest," Janie said. "Six feet under."

"No," Sam chuckled. "He means rest now, here. And help with your burdens."

She laughed, but her heart didn't seem to be in it. "No offense, Sam, but I'm handling my burdens just fine."

"Then why are you so soul weary?"

"Soul weary?" Janie asked. "Who says I'm soul weary?"

"I just have this feeling. Jesus said that he came to give us abundant life—he meant you too, Janie."

"What does that mean? Abundant life?"

"Life so full that it just runs over."

"My life is running over, all right. I have spills all over the place."

"But it could be running over with living water." The words surprised even him.

Now she was quiet as she mulled that over. The toughness in her face seemed to melt away, and she seemed to have trouble speaking. "Living water, huh? Abundant life? Rest?" He wasn't sure, but he thought she was blinking back tears. "Tell you the truth, those sound pretty good."

His heart jolted. Had the Scripture, even poorly quoted,

really gotten to her? Was it possible that she was receptive to Jesus despite his sorry attempt to help her? Maybe he really could do this!

"See . . . I sometimes lie awake at night," she was saying, "and have to get up so early, and I'm so tired—"

"Why do you lie awake nights?" he cut in.

Her eyes grew distant. "I just lie there, thinking."

"About what?"

"About everything falling apart." Her eyes widened as she realized he had said that a moment earlier. "I just keep thinking that nothing's ever going to get better, that things will just keep breaking down until they get worse and worse and worse."

"What things?" he asked.

She covered her eyes and shook her head. "I can't believe I'm talking to you like this." She drew in a deep breath. "My life," she said. She looked down at the wood grain on the table, then brought her moist eyes back to his. "I'm supposed to be cheering you up. That's what you tip me for."

"You do cheer me up," he said. "But if it's all an act, then what's in it for you?"

Her grin faded to aggravation. "No offense, Sam, but what do you care? You come in here every single day, and you've never said more than, 'Hi, how are you?' and I ask if you want the usual, and you say, 'Yes,' and then you eat, and pay me, and go."

"Well, maybe that was the old me."

She laughed again. "The old you? You mean there's a 'new, improved you'?"

"Let's just say there's a new me. I don't know if it's improved or not. Time will tell." If she only knew, he thought.

"And what do you blame this newness on?" she asked sarcastically.

He knew she was teasing him, but it didn't matter. "Jesus Christ," he said.

She rolled her eyes and nodded as if she'd heard it all before. "No, really."

He smiled. "Yes, really. I'm serious. I've been a Christian for a few years now. But last night something happened. I had a dream."

"A dream?" she repeated. "What happened in your dream?"

He leaned forward on the table. She didn't look away. "The Lord spoke to me. He started making me care about the condition of people's souls. And today I've found out that there are frightened souls, empty souls, guilty souls, tired souls . . ."

Her eyes filled up with tears, and she looked away. He had never seen her cry before. He didn't know if he was going to cry now too, but something about those incipient tears grabbed his heart. He didn't know what to say next. He wished his wife was here, so she could try this from a woman's perspective. He wished he had his Bible or a tract that he could toss at her and run.

He was shaking, fearful that he'd upset her more, but he made himself speak. "Janie, don't you want that rest?"

"If I understood how it could happen, I'd take it in a minute," she said. "But just because the Bible said it doesn't mean it's true."

"Because the Bible said it is the *best* reason to believe it's true."

"You believe that?" she asked.

He nodded.

"So what do I have to do? Start going to church? Change how I dress? Do my hair different? Quit going out with men?"

He shrugged. "Hey, do I look like I have a list of rules on me?"

"Isn't that what Christianity is about? Rules?"

"No way. It is not a list of dos and don'ts. It's about God choosing you because he loves you."

"*Choosing* me?" she asked. "Heaven forbid that God should choose me for anything."

He took a bite of his hamburger and chewed. It bought him a couple of minutes. Finally, he spoke again. "Janie, let me tell you how much God loves you."

"Yeah, you tell me," she said, almost mocking.

"Enough to send his only Son to die for you."

She smirked. "See, that's what I don't get. I've never asked anybody to die for me. And when you Christians say that stuff about God sending his only son to die for me, my first question is why? What's the point in that?"

"He died for your sins, and for mine. Because of those sins, we're all destined for hell, but Jesus came to seek and to save that which was lost, and all we have to do is believe in him, and we can change our direction."

"I know an awful lot of people who believe in Jesus," she said. "They're some of the people I drink with at night. Some of the men who try to come home with me. Some of the ones who gamble on the boats. They have 'Honk if you love Jesus' bumper stickers and those little fish symbols on their cars. But they're not a whole lot different from me."

"You got that right."

She squinted at him, obviously surprised. "What?"

"They *should* be different, but you're right about their being a bunch of sinners. Christians are sinners saved by grace."

"And what is that supposed to mean? See, I hear this saved-by-grace stuff on the radio every Sunday, but for the life of me, I can't figure out what it means."

"It means that while we were sinners, Christ died for us, because God promised he would punish sin. We didn't deserve to have Christ pay that penalty for us, and we still don't deserve it. But it doesn't make it any less true. And just because some Christians are hypocrites and just because some of us let God down, it doesn't change any of it. The bottom line is that Christ is true. And he sent me here three times today to talk to you."

She shot him a disbelieving look. "He didn't send you here to talk to me. He sent you for breakfast and lunch."

"Sorry, Janie, but the food's not that good. He sent me because your soul is tired and because there's rest waiting for you."

Her eyes were growing misty again. "Yeah? And how do I get it?"

"By just believing." He shifted in his seat. "Not just recognizing your need, but *clinging* to God to meet your need. Holding on to him for dear life. Embracing him."

"So you're saying that if you believe with all your heart, it makes you different."

"That's exactly what I'm saying. Not a bunch of rules. Just clinging." He smiled and leaned across the table. "The thing is that when you believe, when you really believe, the Holy Spirit will start making changes in you, not because of a list of rules, but because he loves you and wants the very best for you."

"Humph," she said. "I don't know about that." She scratched a spot off of the table with her fingernail. "You know, you ought to be careful. You start talking to somebody like me about God, and the next thing you know, I might actually show up at your church."

"Why would that be a bad thing?"

She shrugged and combed her fingers through the black roots of her bleached hair. "I'm not exactly the kind of person who was raised in Sunday school."

"Neither am I," he said. "Even as a believer, sometimes I'm not the type. But God's working on me. He hasn't given up on me yet, and he hasn't given up on you, either."

She seemed to be considering his words. "So it's not a crush or your stomach that brought you here three times today?"

"Nope. I came because God loves you."

"See, those two things—God and love—don't go together. My picture of God is of a ruler with a big stick, striking down everybody who makes him mad. And I seem to have a knack for that."

"Your picture is wrong. Jesus told a story about a son who took his inheritance and squandered it away on parties and sinful living until he lost everything and had to take a job feeding pigs."

Janie looked around her. "Yep, I can relate to that."

"He realized how much better off he was with his father, so he went back home to ask his father to hire him. He figured his father would never welcome him back into the family, but he hoped he would at least give him a job. But his father saw him coming from a long way off, and he ran out to kiss him. He put a robe and a ring on him and threw this huge party to celebrate his boy's homecoming. That father is the picture of God waiting for you, Janie. Not with condemnation, but with longing and deep love."

For the first time, Janie seemed speechless. Her eyes lit on his for a moment, then darted off, pensive. "If that was true . . . if I could have a love like that . . ."

"You do, Janie," Sam said. "All you have to do is reach out and embrace your waiting Father."

Her eyes blurred with tears, and she wiped them away as they fell.

6

I T WAS MIDAFTERNOON BY THE TIME SAM GOT BACK home, still shaking after his time with Janie. Kate, who got off at three, would be home soon unless her ride didn't bring her straight here. He saw that the light on his answering machine was flickering, so he pushed the button and dropped down on his couch while he listened.

"Hey, Sam, it's me—Bill. Me and the guys'll pick you up at six for the game. Jeff and Steve are coming, but Brother John can't come because he has a meeting tonight. Call me if there's a problem."

Sam sat up quickly. He had completely forgotten about the game he had tickets for tonight. It was the biggest game of the year, between the two biggest state universities. They went every year, but this year was particularly exciting because neither team had lost a game yet.

But then he realized that this wouldn't be like other years. *He* was different.

What would it be like sitting in those stands and hearing all those needy souls around him? He thought of begging off.

He lay down on the couch and tried to take a nap, catch up on some of the sleep he'd lost the night before, but those voices he'd heard today kept circling through his mind. The woman who thought gravity would let her go; the one who thought she was her past; the man who thought he was dirty . . .

He sat up and thought of the people in the houses around him, all of them with voices and needs. What if he could address them all? Help them as he'd helped Janie? He realized this "gift" was going to hound him. But even Christ took time to rest, he thought. Then he berated himself. He had spoken to a few people about Christ today, and now he was patting himself on the back, thinking he deserved a nap. As if he'd addressed multitudes, cast out demons, healed the sick . . .

What was the matter with him? He could do better than he'd done. He didn't have to cower away in his house for fear of hearing what he didn't want to hear. He should see this gift as John saw it—he should look at these as opportunities. He heard the kitchen door shut, and Kate shouted out, "Sam?"

"In here," he called.

She came to the living room doorway, still wearing her nurse's uniform. *She helps people every day,* he thought. *Maybe God should have given* her *the gift.* She would have done a better job of using it. She probably would have never considered using those lottery numbers. "What are you doing home so early?" she asked.

He lay back down on the couch and patted the cushion next to his hip. "Come here," he said.

She approached him slowly. "Are you all right?"

He shook his head. "Sit down." She sat slowly down beside him and touched his forehead. "You're not hot. Are you sick?"

"Sort of. Well, not really." He swallowed and looked up at her. "Remember that dream last night? The one I told you about?"

She nodded. "Vaguely. You were trying to catch a plane . . ."

"No, that was your dream. Mine was the coin. The voice."

"Oh, yeah."

"It did something to me. I mean . . . God did something to me."

"What?"

"He gave me ears . . . to hear. I mean . . . like he hears." Kate's expression reflected her confusion, and Sam sat up, putting his face close to hers. "I know it sounds crazy, but, Kate, you've got to believe me. Call John. He knows. I heard his soul, and then—"

"His soul?" she cut in.

"Yes. And other people's. Everybody I got near today. I heard their spiritual needs. What Christ hears. And John went with me, and we talked to people . . ."

"Went with you where?" She wasn't following him at all.

"To the diner and the hospital."

"You were at the hospital today? My hospital?"

"Yes. But I didn't look you up, because I was a little freaked out, and I didn't know what to tell you about it. But, Kate, we told people about Jesus. Or John did. I just kind of sat there like dead weight. What else is new? But then . . . Janie, the waitress. She accepted Christ today after I talked to her, Kate. And there was this pregnant woman with a little girl and Mrs. Beautral's husband. Did you know she had a husband?"

She was looking at him, as if mentally fitting him for a straitjacket. "No."

"Well, she does, and he had gallbladder surgery, and now he's a Christian."

"Because of his gall bladder surgery?"

"No, because of our visit. Kate, you're not listening!"

She got up and backed away. "Sam, you're scaring me."

"I'm scaring *me*," he said, sitting up. "Kate, I was in the grocery store, and I heard all these voices at the same time. But their mouths weren't moving. I was hearing their souls. Just what the Holy Spirit hears."

"Now I know this is a fantasy," she cut in. "You haven't been to the grocery store in years."

"I went to buy Tylenol. Kate, I'm telling you, I hear things people don't even know they're feeling."

She turned and headed for the kitchen. "I'm getting the thermometer."

"Kate!" He followed her into the kitchen, and as she rummaged through a drawer looking for it, he heard her voice.

"I wish I could have a broken heart again."

"Aha!" he shouted. "You just said you wished you could have a broken heart. I heard you!" His face twisted as he realized the words made no sense. "Why do you want a broken heart?"

She stopped riffling through the drawer and looked up at him. "I didn't say anything about a broken heart."

"You did!" he said. "You did say it. You said, and I quote, 'I wish I could have a broken heart again.'"

Dumbfounded, she closed the drawer and moved across the island from him. "When you say you heard that, what do you mean?"

"In your voice," he said. "I heard it, Kate. It must be in there somewhere, in your soul, even if you don't know it. Even if you wouldn't say it out loud."

Her eyes changed, and her mouth rounded in surprise. "It is."

"See? I told you. What . . . what do you mean, you want a broken heart?"

She seemed to struggle for words that she'd never uttered before. "I've been feeling like . . . like I'm not sensitive to the Holy Spirit anymore. Like I've gotten jaded. Like my zeal has faded. I keep thinking that I need God to break my heart so

I can get back in tune with him. You know, 'Blessed are the poor in spirit. Blessed are those who mourn.' I haven't mourned for Christ in a very long time."

"Yes!" he shouted, jumping. Startled, she backed farther away and grabbed a spatula, as if that would protect her. "Honey, I know just how you feel!"

"And you heard that?" she asked, obviously terrified. "In my voice?"

"I thought it was a curse," he said as tears came to his eyes. He crossed the room and, ignoring the spatula, took her shoulders. "Until I introduced Janie to Christ. And then I came home wiped out, like I'd just recited the Sermon on the Mount to five thousand people. I told *one person* how to know Jesus and I think I'm Elijah."

The shock was beginning to fade, and she looked fully at him now. "You really led someone to Christ?"

"Yes! Can you believe it? *Me!*"

"I've never done that," she said.

"Go with me tonight," he said. "to the game. The guys are picking me up at six, but I'll call them and tell them I'll just meet them there. John isn't using his ticket, so we'll run by and get his, and you can use it."

"You want me at the game?" She touched his forehead again. "You *never* take me to the game. It's guys' night out."

"I want you to come and see. I'll hear the voices. You can help me. Maybe I'll be less of a wimp when you're with me."

"But what'll you tell the guys? They'll think I made you bring me. They'll call you henpecked."

"I don't care what they think. I'll hear their needs too. Maybe I can light a fire under them to help me tell people. Think about it. We could spread out, all of us, and tell people about Jesus until the game's over. We could tell dozens of people about Jesus tonight. We could—"

She grabbed his wrist and began taking his pulse. "You're not going to tell them you hear voices, are you?"

"Well . . . I don't know. They're my best friends. My accountability partners. They can handle it."

"No, they can't," she said, dropping his wrist. "Trust me. You don't want to tell anybody else about this. Just . . . find another way."

"Fine. But will you come?"

"How can I refuse?" she asked. "I'm afraid to let you out of my sight. This could be the prelude to a stroke or something. Is your arm numb, Sam?"

"No," he said. "Kate, I feel great. Nothing is numb. I don't have fever or palpitations. I just have this gift."

She couldn't surrender her worries just yet. Those lines on her face were deep as she stared at him. "I'll come, but I reserve the right to have you committed after the game if I see fit."

He grinned and pulled her into a hug. "Fine. People there need Jesus too."

7

S AM AND KATE SHOWED UP AT THE STADIUM JUST after kick-off. Sam pushed through the crowd of people and up to the section where he and his friends always sat. The three guys were already there, sitting side by side and yelling at the activity on the field. Sam led Kate down the row to the two empty seats.

"Hey, guys, how's it going?"

Bill looked up and slapped hands with him. "Kate, you decided to come out with Sam tonight?"

She gave him a contrite smile. "How will you guys ever forgive me?"

"Man, this is gonna give all of us a bad name," Jeff cut in. "When Andrea finds out that you got to come, next thing you'll know, we'll all have to bring our wives."

Sam glanced at Kate, hoping she wasn't offended. "You know, that wouldn't be the worst thing in the world."

"Look, I'll just go home . . ."

"Kidding," Jeff said. "I was kidding."

But Sam knew he wasn't. He squeezed Kate's hand as they took their seats. He looked down at the field, trying to figure out what was going on. Smathers had the ball and State had just made a first down. A cheer rose up around them, and his friends sprang to their feet.

Then he heard the voices.

"I need a miracle."

Sam looked around, trying to figure out where the voice had come from. It was someone to the left of him, but he couldn't zero in on it.

"I'm gonna die, right here. I'm gonna die and shrivel up."

This came from behind him, and he swung around. All the fans behind him were on their feet, yelling at the top of their lungs.

Next to him, he heard Bill's voice, cracked and high-pitched as he yelled at the referee for making a bad call. But there was another voice coming from Bill. A quieter one that seemed to whisper in Sam's ear. "I can't be used. I'm worthless."

He looked over at his friend, frowning. He couldn't believe that such a dismal thought could come from his soul while he stood on his feet, cheering and yelling at the game before them. Before he could react, he heard another voice from the row in front of him.

"Nothing makes any sense. It's all chance. Coincidence."

Then came the voice of a woman. "I don't know where to go from here. I've forgotten my way home."

None of the faces that went with the voices seemed depressed or dismayed. The people seemed intent on the game, as if it was the one most important thing in their lives. He was amazed at the contrast with what he was hearing from deeper down.

Beginning to feel sick, he realized he was sweating. Kate looked over at him as he unbuttoned his collar.

"Honey, are you okay?" she asked.

He shook his head. "No, I'm not. The voices . . . they're everywhere."

She stared up at him, concern etched on her face. His hands were shaking again. It was like in the grocery store, only worse. The voices were surrounding him, pursuing him. There was no escaping them.

"You want me to go get you something to drink? Or maybe an ambulance?"

"Drink, yes; ambulance, no. I'll come too." He got to his feet, and Jeff leaned around Bill.

"Where you going, man? You just got here."

"I've got a headache, and I—"

The words were like a voice-over, blocking out what Jeff was really saying. "What's the matter with me? Why can't I bear fruit?"

Sam met Jeff's eyes and wanted to answer the question, but he couldn't think. Sudden panic came over him—what would his friend think of his hearing voices? Grabbing Kate's hand, he almost knocked someone down trying to get out of the row, then they walked down the stadium bleachers until they were in the corridor where the concession stands were. There weren't many people there since the game had just begun, so he found a vacant area and hurried to it and leaned back against the wall. Kate was beside him in an instant.

"Sam, something's wrong with you. You're sweating, and you're breathing like you've run a marathon! Are you having a heart attack?"

"No," he said. "It's the voices I told you about. I can hear them everywhere. It's torture."

She stared at him for a moment. Her eyes filled with tears. She covered her mouth with both hands and turned away from him.

He pushed off from the wall and turned her around. "Kate, what's the matter? Why are you crying?"

"Because I don't want you to be crazy," she said in a high-pitched voice.

"I'm not crazy," he said. "Didn't I tell you what you were thinking before?"

"Yes, but . . . this is too weird, Sam. I don't know if I can handle this."

"That's just what I thought. But then I used it, and . . . I can do it again. You'll see. The people out there, they're hurting."

As if his words were further proof that he was nuts, she shook her head. "Those people are cheering at a ball game. Half of them are drunk. They're *not* hurting."

"They *are* hurting," he said. "I heard their pain. I have answers I can give them."

"All right," she said, trying to calm down. She wiped her eyes. "What are we gonna do? Pull them away from the game one by one and tell them what their deepest need is?"

"I don't know," he said. He looked at the few people milling around near the concession stand. "All I know is I'm not gonna accomplish anything standing here." He stepped toward the concession stand, and she followed tentatively. A couple of people were ordering popcorn and hot dogs.

Kate watched him with dread, but he knew her concern had more to do with his health and his mental state than it did with his spiritual gift. She still didn't get it.

"What am I gonna tell my wife?" The voice came from a big man standing close to him. He was munching on popcorn as he waited for his drink order to be filled. "She'll leave me. I'll be alone. I don't know how to fix things."

The words were so personal, so haunting, Sam wished he could just pass out right there on the floor and forget he'd ever heard any of them, but he forced himself to step forward. "Excuse me, but . . . well . . . I have a sense . . . that there's something going on in your life."

The man shot him an annoyed look. "What do you mean?"

"I mean with your wife. You're wondering what you're going to tell her about something, and you're afraid she's going to leave you."

The man caught his breath and took a step back. Kate caught Sam's arm and squeezed, as if to tell him to cool it, that he was about to get decked. "Are you a detective?" the man asked. "Did she hire you?"

The question startled him. "No, nothing like that."

"Because if she did, you can tell her that she's wasting her time. She's not gonna catch me at anything. You got that?"

"Man, this isn't about catching you at something," Sam said. "I don't know what you're involved in. I don't know what's going on with your family. All I know is that you don't have to sit here and wonder what it's going to feel like to be alone."

The man's face twisted. The concession worker brought his drink, but the man didn't see him. "That'll be six bucks," he said, holding out his hand. The patron ignored him and kept staring at Sam.

"Turn it over to God," Sam said. "Believe in him and he'll . . . uh . . . he'll direct your paths." Sam vowed to brush up on his Bible as soon as he had the chance.

Finally, the man realized that the concession attendant was waiting for his money, and he reached into his pocket, got out six dollars, and slapped it on the table. Before getting his stuff, he turned his worried eyes back to Sam. "What has she seen? Have you been following me? Have you got pictures?"

Sam glanced at Kate. Her grip on his arm tightened. "No, nothing like that. I don't even know who you are."

The man gathered his food and turned away. "Look, I've got a game to watch."

"Sure," Sam said, "you go ahead. But remember what I said."

The man started walking faster and faster, until he disappeared around a corner.

Kate caught her breath. "Why did you do that?"

"Because I heard him," Sam said. "He said, 'What am I gonna tell my wife?' That she was gonna leave him and he would be left alone. That's his spiritual need right now. I was trying to address it."

"Well, that was pretty good," Kate said. "Only next time, you might want to pick a guy who isn't built like RoboCop. He could have smashed your face in." She let go of his arm and stared up at him. "I'm sorry, honey, but this is a little strange. People aren't going to accept having you just walk up to them out of the blue like that."

"But I was right. Didn't you see the look on his face?"

"Yes! That's why it was so weird." She lowered her voice as someone walked by. "Sam, do you really think God gave you this?"

"Where else would I get it? I'm not psychic. I'm telling

you, this is real, and it works. Just watch. You can help me," he said. "You and I can both approach people, and you can soften what I say so I won't intimidate them."

She looked as if she was about to cry again. "Sam, you know I want to. But I don't think I can just walk up to someone and start talking like that."

"My emptiness is soul deep," he heard a voice behind him say.

Sam swung around and saw another guy at the concession stand, lurking in front of the candy window, as if that could fill him up.

"If I could turn inside out, I'd just disappear."

Sam's face twisted, and Kate stepped closer. "Did you hear something again?" she whispered.

"Yeah. That guy over there. He said his emptiness is soul deep."

She looked at him, her eyes softening. "That's sad."

"You got that right. Stay here. I'm gonna go talk to him."

Reluctantly, Kate turned to the counter as if trying to decide what to order. Sam got behind the man in the line. "How ya doing?" he asked. He reached out to shake his hand. "My name's Sam. Can I talk to you for a minute?"

"About what?" the guy asked.

"About your soul."

"Oh, brother." The guy rolled his eyes and waved him off as he started to walk away.

"The void is so big that if you turned inside out you'd disappear," Sam blurted.

The man stopped cold and turned slowly around. His mouth fell open, and he tipped his head suspiciously. "Who are you?"

Sam's heart raced. "I'm a friend," he said. "Someone, I think, the Lord sent to talk to you about that void."

The man behind the concession stand leaned over, trying to get the man's attention. "Excuse me. May I help you?"

The man glanced back. "Uh . . . no." He looked back at Sam, surprise in his eyes. "Where do you want to talk?" he asked.

"We could just step right over here," Sam said. "It's as good a place as any."

The man nodded and followed. Kate stayed back, across the corridor, watching with amazement on her face.

The first quarter of the game had almost ended by the time Sam led the man in prayer. He met Kate's eyes and saw that she was crying again. This time she wasn't looking at him as if he was some kind of mental case. She was obviously awestruck.

And so was Sam. The man had been hurting, and he needed to hear what Sam could tell him. He saw Sam as an instrument of divine intervention, and God was answering a prayer that he hadn't even realized he'd uttered.

The two exchanged business cards so Sam could check on

him later, and as the man went back to his seat, Kate came over and reached up to hug him. "That was the most awesome thing I've ever seen."

Sam felt like he was light enough to lift off into the air. "It was pretty awesome, wasn't it? Man, if I'd known it felt this great to introduce somebody to Jesus, I'd have been doing it all along."

"There you are!" someone called.

Sam looked up and saw Jeff coming up the corridor. "Man, we were wondering what happened to you. The first quarter is over. Pratt just scored a touchdown. It was beautiful. You should have seen it."

"I just scored one of my own," Sam said.

Jeff frowned and looked down at Kate, then stepped closer. "What do you mean?"

"I mean I was just standing out here, and there was this guy here, and I started talking to him about Christ, and, Jeff . . . you're not gonna believe this, but the guy accepted him. I prayed with him and everything."

Jeff frowned. "You're kidding me."

"No, I'm not kidding. It happened. Kate saw the whole thing."

Jeff looked down at Kate, then back at Sam. "Man, John's sermon Sunday must have really gotten to you."

He wanted to say that it had gone right in one clogged-up ear and out the other until the Lord himself had spoken, but he just grinned. "You should try it," he said. "Everywhere you look there are people who need Christ. There are so many of them."

"Man, if I did that, atheism would probably soar to all-time highs." He leaned over the concession stand and ordered a drink.

Sam remembered what he'd heard from Jeff in the stands. "You think you can't be used."

Jeff turned back. "Well . . . yeah, I guess so. I mean, I've got a lot of stuff in my past. Even since I became a Christian, there are a few things that would mess up my credibility."

"What's that Jesus said? 'If thy right eye offends thee, cut it out?'"

Jeff grinned. "I've never heard you quote Scripture before."

Sam shrugged. "Man, I've been quoting Scripture all day. Most of it wrong, probably, but at least I'm trying. Did I get that one right?"

"Sounds right."

"All I know is that there aren't enough people out there who know about Jesus. Think how it would change their lives if they knew!"

Jeff was beginning to look uncomfortable. "I wouldn't even know where to begin."

"Just come with me," Sam said. "Hang around here for a minute. You'll see what Kate saw. It's awesome. I'll approach somebody and we can just start talking and . . ."

"Man," Jeff cut in, "I didn't pay forty bucks for this ticket so I could spend the game back here."

Sam tried to hide his disappointment. "Okay, that's fine. We can try it later."

"Fine," Jeff said. He looked irritated as he paid for his drink, then turned back to Sam. "Are you coming back?"

"I don't know," Sam said. "It's a little noisy, and my ears are feeling kind of sensitive."

Jeff shot Kate a look. "Is he sick?"

"I don't think so, Jeff."

He took a sip of his drink and headed back up the stairs. Kate looked up at Sam. "You know, maybe he's not really a Christian. Maybe he just knows *about* Jesus. Maybe he doesn't realize it isn't the same thing as knowing him."

Sam shook his head. "No, I heard his need—it was about bearing fruit. He wouldn't have a need like that if he wasn't a Christian. He just doesn't begin to know how to be used."

"Neither do I."

Sam looked down at her. "Just tell them what Jesus did for you. That's what John told me this morning. That's all it takes. It's not complicated."

"But I can't hear their needs," she said. "I don't have the edge you have."

"Yes, you do. I can tell you what I hear."

A woman walked up to get a straw, and his words trailed off as he heard her voice. "I can't trust anyone. No one can be counted on. I need someone to tell me what to do, but there isn't anyone."

"Talk to her," Sam said, lowering his voice to a whisper. "Go up to her and start a conversation."

Kate looked terrified. "I wouldn't know what to say. What did you hear?"

"She can't trust anyone; she needs someone to tell her what to do. Go on, Kate, talk to her."

"But Sam . . ."

"Kate, God is giving you an opportunity. You're not going to blow it, are you?"

"That's not fair," she said. "He gave you the opportunity, not me."

He shook his head. "No, I'm gonna go over there and talk to that guy in a minute. And if you can talk to her and I can talk to him, in a very short time, we might just lead two people to Christ."

Kate looked over at the woman. She was gathering her food on a tray and was turning to leave. "I can't do it!" she whispered.

Sam looked down at her. "You can honestly know what she's feeling inside, that she's hurting, and not do anything about it? You're a nurse. If she were to drop from a heart attack, you'd bolt forward and do CPR. What is the difference?"

Kate watched as the woman walked over to the other

counter to get ketchup. She shot Sam a look, took a deep breath, and moved toward her. "Excuse me!"

The woman turned around.

"Uh . . ." Kate had an expression on her face that said her mind had gone blank and she couldn't think of another word. "You . . . you look like you have your hands full. I'd be glad to help if I could."

The woman gave her a suspicious look. "That's okay. I've got it. I'm not going far."

Kate glanced self-consciously back at Sam. He winked at her, then started toward the other guy at the counter.

"Look, I know this is weird," he heard her say. "But I just had this sense . . . that you need someone to talk to but you can't trust anyone, and well . . . I know you don't know me from Adam, but I'm a good listener and . . ."

Sam grinned as he reached the man.

"If only someone bigger was in control," the man was saying, "and I wasn't at the mercy of that tyrant I work for."

Sam reached for the straws on the table and accidentally knocked them over. The man squatted and started helping him pick them up. "I've been so clumsy today," Sam said. He extended his hand. "Sam Bennett."

And as they began a conversation, Sam told him who was really in control.

8

S AM DIDN'T RETURN TO THE STANDS UNTIL THE GAME was almost over. His friends, who usually gave each other the benefit of the doubt no matter how bizarre one of them acted, each asked Kate privately if Sam was all right. They were good guys, all of them. The four of them, plus John, their pastor, had become close at a Promise Keepers rally three years earlier. After that, they'd formed an accountability group that met once a week in Bill's office. They prayed for each other diligently and held each other mildly accountable for their Christian walk. But it occurred to Sam as they pushed through the crowd out into the parking lot that none of them had been very fruitful over the years. They'd stayed cloistered in their own little group and had done essentially nothing to reach out to people in need.

As they reached their cars, Kate turned back. "Look, I think I'll just go on home. I'm pretty whipped from working so hard today. Sam, can you ride home with one of the guys?"

Sam shot her a look and started to tell her not to go, but

then he realized he needed this time to talk seriously with his friends.

"I'll take him home," Bill said.

"All right. I'll see you guys later." She reached up and pressed a kiss on Sam's lips, then whispered, "Be careful." He watched her as she got into the car, then he rejoined his friends. "So what's this about you standing in the corridor the whole game, leading people to Christ?" Bill asked as they headed to his car.

"Man, I know it sounds crazy, and you probably won't believe it. But I've just had the most incredible day. I took the day off today and spent it with John. We met all these people and visited in the hospital. He was telling people about Christ left and right, and I got in on the act. It was the most amazing thing."

Bill's eyes twinkled as he took in the story. "It sounds great, man, but do you really think somebody who prays a prayer in a football stadium really knows what they're getting into?"

Sam frowned. "What do you mean 'what they're getting into'?"

"Don't you think you're selling them an easy believe-ism? A repeat-after-me kind of faith?"

"That's not what I'm doing," Sam said. "They need Jesus Christ, and I'm trying to show them where they can find him."

"I'm sorry," Bill said. "I don't mean to be a wet blanket. I just think that sometimes when things come that easy, maybe they really haven't come at all." They reached his car and he unlocked the door. All the guys climbed in.

"All I know," Sam said, settling into the backseat next to Jeff, "is that we meet once a week and we talk about God and all the things he's doing in our lives, and we ask for prayer for each other, and we do devotionals, but how many of us have really influenced anyone else?"

They were all quiet as Bill pulled into the line of traffic waiting to leave the stadium. "There's a harvest out there, and God needs workers," Sam said.

"I just believe I can influence people with my life," Steve said, looking over his shoulder. "At work, people know I'm different. They tell me all the time, and then I'm able to share with them that God is the difference."

"How many times has that happened?" Sam asked, genuinely wondering. "I'm not criticizing, really. Just curious. How many times has someone come up and asked you what's different about you?"

Steve thought for a moment. "Well, last year, people commented on how I behaved when Joan had cancer. Several people mentioned it."

"And what did you tell them?" Sam asked.

"I told them I relied on my faith to get me through."

"Did you tell them about Jesus? Did you pray with them?"

"No, I didn't have to."

"Are those people Christians today?"

Steve was getting angry. "What are you trying to do, man? Pick a fight?"

Sam sighed. "No, nothing like that. I'm trying to point out to you how lame it is just to hope that somebody will figure it out by the look on our faces." The other two guys were acting peeved, too, so Sam backed off for a moment as Bill pulled into the Shoney's parking lot. They were quiet as they went in. Sam closed his eyes, wishing he couldn't hear the waitress's soul saying how powerless and worthless she was. He tried to block out the sound of the man he passed who thought no one cared about him, or the mother who thought life was too chaotic, or the girl whose fear was an overwhelming dread in her heart, or the old man who rued the fact that he could never make anything of himself. All the needs, all the fears, all the dread, all the emptiness. His eyes burned with emotion as he reached the table and sat down.

There are so many people in here, he thought. *I would never have time to go to them one by one and address their needs.* He needed helpers. He needed others to share the burden.

They sat down and the other three guys quietly began looking at the menu. "Look," Sam said. "Look around you at everyone in here. That girl over there, she's scared to death. Feels like life is just too big for her, pressing down on her and she can't breathe."

Bill glanced over at the girl. She didn't look hopeless at all. "What are you talking about?" he asked.

"And that old man over there," Sam said, "he thinks he'll never make anything of himself."

"Well, if he hasn't already," Jeff said, "then he probably never will."

"He can realize that God has already made him valuable by creating him in God's image, that he's special because somebody died for him. He can be a saint and a joint heir with Christ. We have that information. Why are we withholding it from him?"

"Withholding?" Steve asked. "Come on, Sam. You're being a little melodramatic."

"Somebody needs to tell him, Steve," Sam said. "And see that woman over there? She thinks nobody cares about her. She feels all alone. And the waitress who brought us to the table feels completely insignificant."

Steve looked at him with disgust. "How do you know these things?"

"I just know," Sam said. "Every single person in here has a spiritual need. Take you three for instance . . . you need to be fruitful and do the work that Christ started. But no, you don't do it. And so your need isn't being fulfilled. You're the one standing in your own way. Not the church, not your jobs, not anything. Just you."

Bill looked down at the menu, his jaw popping. Steve

stared across the table at him, still disgusted. Next to him, Jeff began tapping his fingers. "Sam, we just wanted to go out and have a good time. Watch a ball game. Crack a few jokes. Why do you have to make this so heavy?"

"Because people are dying," Sam said. "There's a hell and it's real and people are going there. Someone in this room may not make it home tonight."

Bill slammed his hand down on the table. The patrons around them looked up. "Since when are you so worried about people's souls?" he whispered harshly.

"It should have happened when I became a Christian," Sam said. "But it actually didn't happen until this morning."

"So let me get this straight," Steve said. "You went out with John this morning and told a few people about Christ, and now you think you're the apostle Paul?"

"No, I don't think anything like that," he said. "I'm a Christian. Bottom line. That's it. That's all there is."

The waitress interrupted and took their orders, and Sam looked up at her, desperately wanting to tell her that she was valuable, that she was precious in the sight of her maker. But he was in the middle of making a point with his friends, and he couldn't decide which was more important.

She went around the table and took their orders for coffee and soft drinks. When the waitress had scurried away, he looked around at each of them. "Let's make a plan," he said. "Tomorrow night, we drop whatever we're doing, we go out

to the mall or a Laundromat or the hospital, somewhere . . .
and we start talking to people about Jesus."

They each looked at him as if he'd just suggested going for
a swim in a sewer.

"I have a Boy Scout meeting with my son tomorrow
night," Bill said. "I can't go with you."

He looked at Jeff. "What about you?"

Jeff shook his head. "No, I told Andrea I'd be home
tomorrow night. After being out tonight and choir practice
Wednesday night . . ."

"Bring her with you," Sam said. "She'll love it. She'll really
get into it."

Jeff compressed his lips. "I said no, Sam. Not tomorrow."

Sam looked at Steve across the table. "Come on, Steve,
you can come with me."

Steve shook his head. "I'm sorry. I'm just . . . not ready for
that."

"Ready for that?" Sam asked. "What do you mean?"

"I mean, I'm not prepared. I don't know what to say to
people. You know, I have considered taking that evangelism
class John told us about Sunday, maybe learning a few verses
of Scripture, practice a little, learn how to share my faith
before I actually go out there and do it."

"Man, you don't need a script." Sam looked from one
man to the next, crushed that he couldn't persuade them. "If
you could just *hear* what's going on in people's hearts!"

Bill gaped at him. "Like you can?"

Sam wanted to tell them, but he knew they'd never believe it. "Bill, it's our job to go out and tell people."

Bill blew out a sigh, then looked at his watch. "It's getting late, and I'm tired."

Sam stiffened. "We didn't get our drinks yet."

"I know, but I'm getting a headache." Bill got to his feet. "Let's just go."

"Am I making you that uncomfortable?" Sam asked. "Man, I've looked you in the eye and questioned your parenting. I've challenged you about your prayer life. I've held you accountable for your language. You've never gotten hot at me before. Why now?"

Bill sat back down and rubbed his face. "I'm not mad, Sam. I just don't quite get where this is coming from."

"Maybe . . . God? Ya think?"

The other men kept their eyes riveted on his, and suddenly Sam realized he was going about this all wrong. He didn't need to shame them into talking about Jesus. What he needed to do was get them excited, fill them with stories about what had happened to him today. The joys and the victories. "Guys, just listen for a minute. I want to tell you about some of the people I talked to today. Just open your minds and listen."

The waitress came back with their drinks, and the four of them sat there as Sam went on and on about the pregnant woman with the little girl, and Janie, the waitress, and the man tonight who had wept and accepted Christ at the stadium. At last he ran out of stories, and they sat, uncomfortably quiet.

He wondered if he should give up. "I've really put a damper on the whole night, haven't I?"

"No, it's just late." Bill's voice was flat. "I'm tired. Need to get home."

"All right." He got up and followed them wearily to the car. They got in one by one, none of them saying a word. Sam was the first one Bill took home. When they pulled into his driveway, Sam waited a moment before getting out. "Guys, I'm really sorry for coming on so strong tonight, but this is serious business." He hesitated, waited for some kind of response, but there was only silence. He opened the door. When it was clear that they were all waiting for him to get out, he did. "See you guys later," he said in a weak voice.

They muttered their good-byes, and he closed the door. He drew in a deep breath and let it out slowly as he walked to the front of his house. "Help them, Lord," he whispered before he went inside. "Work on them like you worked on me. Give them a chance to know this joy."

9

KATE WAS ALREADY IN BED WHEN SAM CAME IN. HE leaned down and kissed her cheek. She smiled and hugged him. "John called. Said he needs to talk to you, no matter how late."

"Good."

"How did it go with the guys?"

Sam began unbuttoning his shirt. "They may never speak to me again."

"Why not?"

"Because I made them uncomfortable." He sank down on the mattress next to her and slumped over with his elbows on his knees. "Oh, Kate. I was awful. I was sarcastic and accusing . . . No wonder I didn't make any headway with them."

"You should have just witnessed to someone else right there in front of them, like you did me. Let them overhear you telling someone about Jesus. That would have done it."

"Yeah," he said, regretting the missed opportunities.

"There was a waitress in Shoney's who really had a deep need. I was too distracted with them, so I didn't talk to her."

"You can go back tomorrow."

"Yeah." He got up. "I'd better let you sleep. You have to get up early."

She turned over to go back to sleep, and Sam went into the living room, too revved up for bed. It was just after ten. He wondered if John was still awake. He was glad the pastor needed to talk. He could use an ear himself.

He dialed John's number.

"Hello?"

"John? It's me, Sam."

"Hey, Sam. I just wanted to touch base with you and see how things are going. Kate said you'd been turning the stadium upside down."

"Yeah," he said, as the joy began to return. "Man, you should've been there. Tonight at the ball game, I kept hearing the voices. It was driving me crazy, so I went to the concession area and started talking to people as they came by."

"All by yourself?" John chuckled. "This morning you were scared to death to talk to strangers."

"Yes," he said, "but you helped me through it. Then I got Kate involved and she started doing it."

John began to laugh, and Sam grinned. "What is it?"

"I don't know why I'm always so surprised when prayers are answered," John said.

"You prayed about this?"

"I pray for all of you, all the time. I pray and beg and plead with God to give us revival so our members will be bold about sharing their faith, and now this is happening. I feel like a teenaged boy who just got a new car or something. Do you realize what could happen to our church because of this? If other people start to catch your zeal, and people are led to Christ, and—"

"Well, don't get too excited," Sam cut in. "It doesn't seem to be working like that."

"What do you mean?"

"Well, tonight, I told Bill, Jeff, and Steve about all the people I'd talked to today and how I was feeling."

"Did you tell them about the voices?"

"No," he said. "I didn't think they could handle that. You gotta admit, that's like something out of the Twilight Zone. I just told them your sermon Sunday got to me and that I had started to feel an urgency."

"That's good," John said.

"And true. But the problem is, they weren't that interested. In fact, they're pretty steamed at me right now. All of them."

"Why?"

Sam shook his head. "I told them all about what I had come to understand today. I told them about the people we had visited and what had happened. They just sat there looking at me like I was crazy, like they were upset that I would have the gall to tell them about this."

"It challenged them," John said. "I can get away with it from the pulpit, but one on one, face to face, they don't like it very much."

"But I heard their needs, John. I heard what they feel. That they need to be used. It's something they want. The Holy Spirit in them is crying out to do something."

"But their flesh is so weak, they don't realize they want it," John said.

"They had all these excuses. Boy Scouts and time with their wives—which never kept them from doing anything before—and fear of saying the wrong thing. It was the most amazing thing I've ever seen."

"Doesn't surprise me," John said. "I deal with it every day. Ninety-nine percent of the congregation is just like them."

"What about this evangelism class you mentioned?" Sam asked. "Didn't it start yesterday?"

"Yeah." John sounded underwhelmed.

"Well, how did it go? Maybe I could call on some of them."

John was quiet as he seemed to consider that. "I had high hopes for that class," he said. "I thought the preparation would shoot through some of their excuses. I thought maybe I'd have a couple dozen people show up, but it didn't work out that way."

"How many did you have?"

"Just a handful. *Less* than a handful."

"Well, still. That's some. Maybe I could call them and they could go out with me tomorrow night."

"All right," John said. "I'll give you their names. They're people who really do want to be fruitful. Maybe they'll agree to go." By the time he got off the phone with John, Sam realized it was too late to call anyone else. He set his list by the phone for the next day, then fell into bed, exhausted, and thought about the dream that had plagued him the night before. He wondered if he would dream tonight. He wondered if, when he woke, that gift would still be there.

But the next morning, when he got up, he realized it was still there when he heard Kate's voice yearning for another person to lead to Christ today. Not able to make himself wait longer, he began to call down the list John had given him. The first person he reached told him he couldn't go out, that he was afraid and was hoping that the class itself would help him with the fear factor.

"Words don't come easy for me," the man said. "I just would feel better if you could wait a couple of weeks."

The next person said something similar. "I've already got plans tonight. Tickets to the musical. My wife would kill me if I backed out."

One by one, he went down the list of hopefuls, and

though his call was met with a little more interest than he had seen the night before, he had the distinct impression that these people were terrified of doing what he had done yesterday. Was there no one in the church who would help him with this harvest? No one other than the preacher?

He took Kate to work and headed to the diner to get breakfast, wondering if Janie had changed her mind overnight or forgotten their talk yesterday. But as he walked in, he could see that something was different in her. She was beaming, and she looked rested. It was clear that Christ was still with her. The normal chaos in the diner seemed more settled today, and even the cook was quieter.

He took a place at the counter and waited to hear the voices that would bombard him as soon as anyone got near. Janie came rushing up to him the moment she spotted him. "Hi, Sam. Listen, I tried to call you last night, but you weren't home. I needed to ask you something."

"Sure, what?"

"My sister. I want to tell her what you told me yesterday, only I'm afraid I don't know what to say. I want her to know Jesus too, and I was wondering if you would come with me to talk to her. I mean, I'll do the talking, but I thought it might be better if you came along so that if she has questions, or if I do, you'll be there to answer them. There's nothing worse than me trying to explain something I don't completely understand myself."

He looked up at her, his eyes bright with emotion. "Janie, I would be honored."

"Can you do it tonight after you get off work? I told her I was gonna come about seven."

"Yes, I can come then."

"Then, if it's not too much trouble, I wondered if you would come with me to the restaurant where my son works as a waiter. He takes a break at nine o'clock, and I was really hoping that we could talk to him and some of his friends . . ."

Sam couldn't believe it. He'd spent all last night and this morning trying to find someone in his church to help him with the harvest, and already one of his fruits from yesterday was anxious to reproduce. Was this the way it was supposed to work? he thought. Maybe it was.

"I tell you what, if you don't think it'll be too many people, I'll bring Kate with me tonight too. Then if we need to split your son and his buddies up and talk to them one on one, there'll be more of us to go around."

Janie was almost dancing as she considered that. "Meet me here at six-thirty, and we'll head out," she said. "This is gonna be so much fun!"

10

ONCE AGAIN, SAM WAS EARLIER TO WORK THAN MOST of the people in his building. His secretary wasn't in yet, but someone had made coffee. He poured himself a cup, then went into his office. He dug through the bottom drawer of his file cabinet and took out his Bible. An old church bulletin marked his place, but he couldn't remember the last time he'd read from it.

There was so much he needed to know, he thought. So much that still eluded him about Christ. People would ask. He needed to be prepared. He wished he'd memorized more Scripture. He wished he'd hidden it in his heart.

A new hunger to know the Word overwhelmed him, and he began to read, marking passages and writing in the margins, trying to commit verses to memory. He didn't notice as the employees began to fill the building and the work day officially began. So when someone knocked on his door, he was startled. He looked up and saw his boss, Rob

Simpson, with one of his biggest advertising clients standing behind him.

"Sam, I thought you might like to know that Mr. Hagle is here."

Sam got up and came around the desk, extending his hand. "Mr. Hagle, it's great to see you."

"Sorry I missed you yesterday," the man said. "I took Rob to lunch."

"I wasn't feeling well," Sam said. "Long story, but I'm better today."

The man glanced at Sam's desk. "What's that you're reading?"

"The Bible," Sam said. He looked at his clock and realized eight o'clock had come and gone. "Guess it's time to be putting that up."

He heard a voice coming from the client, though his lips only moved in small talk. "I wish there was something in there for me. Light at the end of my tunnel."

Sam seized the opportunity to pounce before he could lose his nerve. "You know, Mr. Hagle, I don't know if you've ever read the Bible. If you haven't, you ought to give it a try. It sure does add light to the end of a long, dark tunnel."

The man's face changed. Frowning, he locked eyes with Sam. "I'll keep that in mind."

Sam nodded. Rob hurried the client out of the room, and Sam stepped into the doorway and watched until they'd turned the corner. Sam went back to his desk, closed his Bible, and put it away. He began working on the account that was sitting on his desk, calling for his attention. After a few moments, the phone buzzed. He picked it up. "Sam Bennett."

"Sam, this is Rob. I want to see you in my office. Now."

Sam closed his eyes. Maybe he had made a mistake mentioning the Bible and his faith to a client. Was Rob about to chew him out? He hurried to his boss's office and knocked on the door. He heard a gruff, "Come in."

Slowly, he walked inside. "You wanted to see me?"

"Yeah, I wanted to see you," Rob said, leaning back in his chair. "I want to talk to you about what just happened."

"What did just happen?" Sam asked, taking the chair across from his desk.

"I bring a client by your office, and you're sitting there reading the Bible, of all things. And as if that isn't bad enough, you have the gall to start telling him that *he* needs to be reading it." Rob got to his feet and began pacing back and forth across the office. "How do you think that makes the company look? How much faith do you think that man's going to put in us, when he sees you soaking up a bunch of superstitious philosophies and telling him *he* needs to do it?"

Heat rushed to Sam's face. "Look, Rob, I didn't know you were coming to my office. I came in here early this morning and started reading. The time got away from me."

"You were reading it on our time," Rob said. "It wasn't your time—it was our time. You never know when a client's going to stop by. You can't let them catch you doing something so stupid—"

"It was not stupid," Sam said, springing to his feet. "That is God's Word, not some stupid, superstitious philosophy, as you refer to it." It was the first time he'd lost his temper with his boss, and he knew he was getting dangerously close to losing his job.

Then he heard the voice, coming from Rob's soul, deep within him, too loud to ignore. "I can't stand my life anymore."

The words stopped Sam cold.

"My tunnel's so dark and so long that it's already swallowed up all the light."

Sam's anger vanished, and he looked into his boss's eyes and felt a compassion that he hadn't felt before. "Rob, the light can't be swallowed up."

Rob shot him a disgusted look. "What are you talking about? What light?"

"The light at the end of the tunnel," he said. "The darkness is never gonna swallow the light, because it's God's light and it's there, in his Word."

"It's a book!" he yelled. "Just words on a piece of paper, and I don't want it in my company. I will not have it ruining the credibility that we have with our clients. Either you get that through your head or you pack up your office and get out of here."

Sam realized that his boss was hurting. Something was going on in his life, and since he couldn't read his thoughts, but only the general emptiness of his spirit, he didn't have a clue what it could be. He grabbed a pad from Rob's desk and began to write.

"What are you doing?" Rob demanded.

Sam tore the page off and handed it to Rob. "This is my home number. I want you to call me any time you want to talk. I mean any time, night or day. Two in the morning. I don't care."

"Why would I call you in the middle of the night?"

Sam shrugged. "I don't know. I get the feeling that you need to talk."

"I'm talking right now! I told you to pack up the Bible or pack up your things!"

"I know," he said, "but I'm serious. If you need to talk, call me. Or you could come to church Sunday. I go to Church of the Savior on Post Road. Come and hear more about . . ."

"Get out of my office!"

"All right, Rob. I'm sorry I got you riled up." Before Rob could respond, Sam headed back to his office and closed himself in. He went back to his desk. They could keep him from reading his Bible on company time, he thought, but they couldn't keep him from praying. Quietly, he began to pray for Rob and the spiritual need he'd heard in his soul. As he did, he had a sense of peace, that God was working on Rob just as he'd once worked on Sam.

11

FOR THE REST OF THE WEEK, SAM REVELED IN HIS GIFT. He began to look forward to hearing the voices of the souls in the places he went. He even sought out crowds so that he could have access to more and more people. Kate, too, caught the zeal and began to rush home after work so they could go out to eat and find people to talk to.

When Sally, his secretary, didn't win the lottery, she failed to come to work for several days. Concerned about her, he finally paid her a visit.

As he stood on her porch next to the plants that needed watering, waiting for her to answer, he hoped that his gift hadn't been responsible for her withdrawal. He never should have repeated those numbers back to her. If he hadn't, maybe she wouldn't have put so much hope in the numbers being God's gift.

The door squeaked open, and Sally peeked out. Her eyes were red and swollen. "Sam?"

"Sally, are you okay?" Sam asked.

She nodded and swiped at her nose with a tissue.

"Can I come in?" She hesitated for a moment, then reluctantly stepped back to let him in.

"I wasn't expecting company," she said, "now that I'm not a millionaire." She said the words as if she'd been robbed of her fortune and all her friends had fled.

"It's fine," he said, stepping over wadded tissues on the carpet. Boxes of items cluttered the floor—a computer, a new television, a stereo system. Sam looked around and wondered if she had charged them on her credit card, planning to pay them off when her lottery numbers were chosen. The room was dark, as if she had been sitting there, crying and staring at the things she had coveted.

"I had so many affirmations," she said in a hoarse, stopped-up voice as she dropped miserably onto her sofa. "You even repeated the numbers I had in my head. How could that be if they weren't the right numbers?"

Sam realized he had unintentionally led her down the wrong path. He had almost used his gift to go that way himself. "I didn't know the numbers, Sally," he said. "How could I know?"

"But you said them!"

"I just had this feeling . . . about your spiritual condition. That your self-worth was somehow tied up in this lottery. That maybe I was even one of the people you wanted to show your true worth to."

She grabbed another Kleenex and blew her nose. "If I had become a multimillionaire, we'd see who was superior then."

"Why do you want to be superior?"

"Because I'm tired of being inferior. Equal would have even been good. But now I'm still just a peon."

"You've never been a peon, Sally. I couldn't get any of my work done without you."

"You'd hire another secretary in ten minutes flat. I wouldn't even be a fond memory." She began to cry again on the last words and pressed the wadded tissue to her eyes.

"Sally, you don't seem to know how much you mean to God."

"God?" she asked. "What's this got to do with God?"

"God cares more about you than he does some lottery ticket."

"Obviously he cares *nothing* about my lottery ticket. Not a thing. *Less* than nothing!"

"But you're not listening. He cares about you. And he knows you're worth a whole lot more than money. You're worth everything he had to give—Jesus gave his life for you."

"Oh, don't give me that," she bit out. "I know all about the cross. I was raised in church. I'm there every time the doors open. I teach Sunday school. I take food to poor families at Thanksgiving. I know more than you do about Jesus!"

"But knowing about Jesus doesn't do you much good, Sally. The Bible says that you have to 'confess with your mouth that Jesus is Lord, and believe in your heart that God raised him from the dead, and you will be saved.' If you believe in your heart that God did that, Sally, then why can't you trust him with your finances? Why can't you believe that you're worth a lot more than money?"

"Well . . . I do believe that . . . I do."

But Sam could hear her soul, and he knew she didn't really believe it. Not in her heart. They were just words to her, words she'd heard over and over throughout her life. Words that had little meaning to her. In her heart, where it counted, she didn't really believe.

"I just . . . wanted to be rich. If God loved me so much, he would want me to be rich too."

"What makes you think that God's business is making his people rich? Maybe he needs you to stay in the middle class for some higher purpose. Maybe he even needs you poor, so he can use you a certain way. His children have a much higher value than dollars and cents. He has a plan for you that's better than any winning lottery ticket."

She was getting angrier. "If you weren't my boss . . ."

"What? What if I weren't your boss?" Sam waited.

She threw her chin up. "If you weren't my boss, I'd grab you by the throat and throw you out of my house!"

"Why?" he asked.

"Because you've got a lot of nerve, preaching to me. I'm one of the pillars of my church. I don't need you coming in here telling me about Jesus in my time of grief."

Sam got up, his hands innocently outstretched. "I've offended you—I didn't mean to do that. I just thought you should know that Jesus cares about you."

"I do know. I guess you're gonna fire me now. Kick me while I'm down!"

"No, I'm not going to fire you," he said. "I'm going to pray for you. That you'll understand how precious you are to God."

"I'll show you," she said. "I'll show you all. I'll win that lottery next week. If I buy enough tickets, I'm sure to win one of these times. I'm not one to give up this easy!"

Sam left her house and got back into his car, feeling sick that he hadn't been able to do better than that. *This is hard,* he thought. He closed his eyes and dropped his forehead onto the steering wheel. "Lord, please help Sally. My coming to see her was not enough. You've got to draw her to you. I can't do any of this by myself. Without you there with me, my words are empty. Useless."

When he started his car and looked back up at her door, he had tears in his eyes. Humbled, he drove off, aware more than ever that this gift had its limitations.

But Sam didn't let his visit with Sally stop him and decided to depend more than ever on the Holy Spirit to lead him. He lost count of the number of people he led to Christ, as well as the number who rejected him outright. The more he told, the more he wanted to tell, and the greater the urgency in his soul grew.

He couldn't wait until Sunday so he could try to appeal

to some of his Christian friends at church to get out there with him. He had been praying earnestly and diligently about it, as Kate had, and he had faith that the Lord would provide helpers for the harvest.

Sunday morning, he and Kate went to the Waffle House for breakfast and shared the gospel with an old man who was sitting there alone. It almost made them late for church, but they pulled into the parking lot just as the organ music began to play. Sam hurried into the foyer, then through the double doors into the sanctuary.

And he stopped cold. The church was packed. He realized he had never seen it this full since they'd completed the new building three years earlier, not even on Easter. They had built it hoping for church growth, but the numbers had declined since that time. Today, however, every pew was full, and folding chairs had been brought in at the back. Even the balconies had people in them.

He looked at Kate and saw that her eyes were glowing. Taking her hand, he slipped into a back pew as the congregation rose and began to sing. The pastor stood at the front of the room, beaming with excitement and joy. Sam looked around him as they sang. There, across the room, he saw Janie, the waitress, with her sister who had accepted Christ a few days before. Down the row was her son with two of his friends.

Kate nudged him and he followed her gaze across the aisle. It was the woman she'd spoken with at the ball game the other night. Two rows in front of her was one of the people he'd met at a convenience store. His eyes scanned the crowd, and up toward the front he saw Sid Beautral, from the hospital, and his wife. The man looked weak, but his face was full of joy.

When the praise time ended, John began to preach the sermon that was so much like the previous Sunday's. But last Sunday no one had heard. He talked about Luke 15 again, about the lost coin and the lost sheep and the lost son—he said that they were all things that others might have shrugged off as insignificant, but Jesus saw them as important enough to stop everything to seek them. As John preached, Sam prayed silently that the other Christians in the room would hear and respond, that their hearts would be opened to their true potential—reaching a lost world.

"I'm going to do something different today," John said. "I can't help thinking that some of you here would like to profess God before men. We're going to have an altar call, and I want you to come if you feel convicted to share what Christ is doing in your life." This time, Sam didn't check his watch as he had the week before. Instead, he continued to pray, not caring if anyone saw his eyes closed.

Kate nudged him again, and he looked up. A crowd was forming at the front of the room as the people sang on. He strained his neck to see who had gone forward. He saw Janie and her sister and her son, the lady at the ball game, Sid Beautral, and countless others they had met that week.

His eyes began to fill, and he covered his mouth and began to weep. Kate was already crying as if her heart was broken, but he knew the joy that bubbled in her soul as she clung to him. As the music leader led them in another verse, he hoped they wouldn't end the altar call yet. There were others, he knew, more of them who needed to make commitments. They needed another verse. Another song. Another hour. He sang clear and loud, his voice reaching out a prayer of thanks and supplication to his Father.

And then he saw another man slip out of the aisle and head down to the front.

"Anyone you know?" Kate whispered.

He wiped the tears from his face and narrowed his eyes to see through the blur. As the man turned to the side to whisper to John, Sam realized who it was. "That's Rob. My boss."

Kate stood on her toes to see over the heads. As Rob began to weep, head to head with John, Sam had to restrain himself from leaping forward and running down the aisle himself. Then another came, and another, and at last, he realized that almost as many heard the gospel from Kate as from him or John. People began moving from the front pews to make room for those who had come down. It was a marvel he hadn't been prepared for.

When John was satisfied that no one else was going to come, he nodded to the minister of music and they closed the song. Finally, when the music had stopped, John went back to the pulpit with a tear-stained face.

"Brothers and sisters," he said in a voice full of emotion, "I want to introduce some people to you. They've each accepted Christ this week, and the story is the same over and over. A handful of these I spoke with, but the rest of them were led to Christ and invited here by either Sam Bennett or his wife, Kate."

Sam hadn't expected to be mentioned, and as heads turned and people sought him out, he looked at the floor, unable to meet their eyes. He didn't want the recognition, he thought. He just wanted help from other Christians.

"Sam?" John said from the pulpit.

Sam looked up.

"Would you come up here for a minute, please?"

Sam had no idea what John wanted him to do, but he got up, wiped his face, and walked the aisle. He went up to the pulpit and stood next to John, his face wet with his tears.

"Something's happened to Sam this week," John said. "This past week, he started listening to people's needs. One by one, he and Kate led these people here today. But they need help. I want to ask you, those of you who want to be like Sam, who want to help change people's lives, come to my class today at 4:00. Let's learn some Scripture you can use when sharing your faith, talk about ways to seek out the people who need to hear. Let's figure out how we can tap into Christ's vine to make our own branches bear fruit. And please come up and welcome our new brothers and sisters."

Then, one by one, he began to introduce those who had come, welcoming them to the family of God, embracing each one of them. Sam was there to accept the hugs and thanks of all who had come. When Rob came up, Sam reached for his hand. Rob pulled him into a hug. "Thank you," he whispered, overcome.

"You didn't call," Sam said. "I haven't even seen you at work."

"I've been thinking about it all week," Rob said. "I couldn't stop thinking about what you'd said. You may have saved my life. I owe you, big time."

"No," Sam said. "It's not me you owe."

By the time everyone had been welcomed and greeted and most of the congregation had left the church, Sam was exhilarated. A handful of people lingered behind.

Lawrence Shipman, the chairman of the deacons, approached him with a concerned look on his face. "What are you doing to get these people into church?" he asked. "Bribing them? Offering them food? What?"

Sam hadn't expected a question like that. "I've been telling them about Jesus."

"I want to know what they expect," he demanded as if he hadn't heard Sam, "coming here and bringing all their friends like that. Do they think they're gonna get something out of it?"

"They'd be right if they think that," Sam said. "They are gonna get something out of it."

"But some of these people don't fit in with our congregation," Lawrence said. "Did you see how some of them were dressed? Like they'd come straight from a bar. Church may not be the place where they need to be."

Sam's face began to grow hot as it had with Rob in the office the other day. He opened his mouth to tell Lawrence that people with his attitude were the reason for the stagnant state of their church for the past few years. But before he could formulate the words, he heard the man's inner voice. "I'm powerless. I don't have any control."

Sam's anger vanished. "Lawrence, there isn't a person on the face of the earth who wouldn't be welcome in this sanctuary, as far as I'm concerned."

"We have to exercise some kind of decorum. These people can't just sluff in here wearing tennis shoes and torn up blue jeans and bleached hair with black roots. Look around. That's not how we look."

"No, we wear all our sins on the inside, don't we? Packed away nice and tight, in clean little packages."

The man looked as if Sam had just slapped him across the face.

"Lawrence, I know you feel kind of powerless right now, but we're not supposed to be in control. God is. It's his house, not ours."

"Powerless? This isn't about power!"

"Of course it is," Sam said. "There are people at this church who would rather die than give up their power to the Holy Spirit."

"John!" Lawrence raised his voice, summoning the pastor over. John turned from talking to two other deacons and joined them. "You can't just stand there and let this happen. They're gonna ruin our church and change the whole face of our congregation."

John grinned from ear to ear. "I should hope so, Lawrence. I've been trying to do that myself for a long time. It looks like the Holy Spirit has decided to answer my prayers."

Lawrence shook his head and muttered something about calling a deacons' meeting and bringing this before the out-reach committee. Then with a red face, he stormed out of the sanctuary.

John's expression lost its joy as he watched the man leave. "What did you hear in that, Sam?"

Sam shook his head. "I don't think he's a Christian."

"He thinks he is, though," the pastor said. "The Pharisaical kind. Setting a bunch of rules, but forgetting the relationship."

Sam set his hand on John's shoulder. "Don't let him ruin it for you, John."

John's face slowly lit back up. "I won't. Sam, thank you for helping with the greatest Sunday I've ever had in the pulpit."

"I just did what you taught me and what the Holy Spirit gifted me to do."

"Then you'll be back this afternoon to visit with the class?"

"I sure will," John said. "And let's pray for some of them to help us out."

But that afternoon, there were only eight at the evangelism class, and they all still had reasons why they weren't ready to talk to others about Jesus just yet. Still, they couldn't help being inspired by the number of people who had come down that morning. One of them suggested that they plan a "Let Us Rejoice" party for Friday night and invite the whole church to celebrate with the new believers, as the angels in heaven rejoiced. John thought it was a wonderful idea and an excellent opportunity to baptize them.

"We'll have to have food, lots of food," John said. "Kate, would you mind heading that up?"

"Not at all," she said. "We may not be able to recruit people to witness, but they're always willing to make food."

Sam didn't have much to say about the party. His joy in introducing people to Jesus was at an all-time high. He didn't see a reason for celebrating when there were still so many people out there who didn't know Christ. So many needs. So many people hurting. Every moment he spent with people afraid to be obedient to the command to evangelize the world was a moment that he was taking from people who needed him. He couldn't wait for the meeting to end so he and Kate could head to the mall.

That night, they led eighteen people to Christ.

Friday night, Sam showed up at the "Let Us Rejoice" party and congratulated all those he'd led to Christ. Modestly, he accepted words of praise for his good work from congregates who'd had several days to think about what he had done. He cried through the baptisms, but when they were finished and the party began, Sam grew restless. There were places he had to go, he thought, people he had to see. Needs he had to hear. He told Kate he was going to slip away, then quickly, he disappeared.

It was the Luke 15 kind of thing, he thought. He had to tear the house up and find that coin. He had to leave the ninety-nine sheep and look for the one. He had to scan the horizon for that lost son.

Tonight, something told him there would be lost sons coming in from out of town.

He drove to the bus station, where he had refused to go with John a few days earlier, and timidly, he walked in. There wasn't a bus there, but several people in the lobby were waiting for one to arrive. He sat down on a bench next to a woman with a baby . . . and began to listen.

But instead of her voice, he heard the sound of his cell

phone ringing. He had started carrying it in his pocket so that anyone he'd witnessed to who might have questions could get in touch with him night or day. Quickly, he pulled it out and answered.

"Sam, this is Bill. Where are you, man?"

He hesitated. Bill, who'd had little to do with him since the game, had been at the party when he'd left. "I'm at the bus station. Why?"

"Because I was just thinking," he said. "Looking around at all these people who look so happy and thinking that never in a million years could I have led any of them to Christ . . ." His voice cracked. "Look, man. The Lord's really been working on me since that game the other night, and I'm thinking that maybe I need to come and help you out."

Sam got slowly to his feet. "Really?"

"Yeah. You got enough to go around? Because Jeff and Steve are standing here with me, and they'd kind of like to come too."

Sam threw his head back and laughed out loud. This was too good to be true. "There's a bus due in twenty minutes," he said. "There'll be plenty for all of us."

"All right, stay put. We're on our way."

A tear rolled down Sam's face as he dropped his phone back into his pocket.

12

Kate was already home when Sam returned that night, and he came in and called out for her. She rushed into the room, her hands on her hips. "How many?" she asked with a grin.

He shrugged. "I can't even say. Some of them listened. Some didn't. But the main thing is that Bill and Jeff and Steve got initiated into the harvest."

"I know!" She clasped her hands and did a little dance. "I couldn't believe it when they told me where they were going. Did *they* have any success?"

"Each of them led at least two people. It was phenomenal. They were practically jumping up and down. You should have seen it. And then I gave Bill a ride home, and all the way he kept thinking of different people he was gonna tell tomorrow. I think it's gotten into his blood now. There's no turning back."

Kate squealed and threw her arms around him. "You know, I have never been so proud of you as I have these last two weeks."

"Well, I'm pretty proud of you too."

"Don't be. I haven't done nearly what you've done."

"Well, like you said the other day, I have an edge."

She sat down, and he told her about some of the people he'd met, their needs, the ways he'd answered them. They laughed and wept and prayed together.

Later, when she went to bed, Sam stayed up. He was too energized to sleep, and he wanted to spend some time with the Lord. Humbly, he got down on his knees and thanked God for the blessing of ears with which to hear, for the needs he was able to fulfill, for the heart of flesh that had replaced his own heart of stone. And then he thanked God for the soul-winners he was raising up among Sam's friends and his brothers and sisters in Christ, and among the babes in Christ who had new stories to tell and new circles of friends who needed to hear.

Then he sank down in his recliner, opened his Bible, and began studying the Scripture. There was so much he had to learn, he thought. His soul soaked up all he read, digesting everything he saw.

Hours later, he fell asleep with the Bible in his lap.

And again, he began to dream . . .

13

HE DREAMED OF THAT LOST COIN, BUT THIS TIME HE was the one searching his house, looking under things and on top of things. And then he heard that divine, powerful voice that he'd heard almost two weeks earlier. But the words were different.

"And lo, I am with you always, even unto the end of the age."

He jolted awake and realized he had fallen asleep in the recliner with his Bible in his lap. He felt as touched by God as he had that first night when he'd wakened in a cold sweat with his hands trembling and his heart pounding. Breathless, he got up and went into the bedroom. Kate was still asleep. He didn't want to wake her, because he didn't know what to say.

Finally, he stepped into the shower and let the water cool and calm him as it rained down on him. When he came out, Kate stirred and looked at the clock. It was 5:00 A.M. "Did you ever come to bed last night?" she asked in a groggy voice.

"No, I fell asleep in the chair," he said quietly. He pulled on his robe and sat down on the edge of the bed. "Kate, I had another dream. I heard God talking to me again."

Kate sat up in bed, her eyes squinted. "What did he say?"

"He said, 'And lo, I am with you always, even unto the end of the age.'"

"Well, that's a nice thought. Right out of the Bible. Jesus said it after he gave the Great Commission."

"Yeah, but why did I dream it?"

"Maybe to remind you of the Great Commission he gave you?"

Sam thought that over as he got dressed and headed early to the diner for breakfast. Since it was Saturday, he left Kate to go back to sleep.

Sam parked in front of the diner and went in. He scanned the patrons as he walked to the counter. Some of them were people he had talked to over the last two weeks. Some of them had prayed with him. Some had even come to his church and the "Let Us Rejoice" party the night before. They looked up at him and smiled, and he gave a cursory wave and went to his usual stool at the counter.

He sat down and glanced to his side, smiled and nodded at the elderly woman next to him.

Janie came up. "Hi, Sam. Ready for the usual?"

"Thanks, Janie."

As she scurried away to get his breakfast, it dawned on him that he hadn't heard any voices yet. He sat up straighter on his stool and swiveled around, looking one by one into the faces of the people closest to him. Normally, he would have heard three or four by now. But even the woman right next to him remained silent. He leaned closer to her and tried to listen. But nothing came. She was eating her bacon, nibbling on a piece of toast, and there weren't any words coming out of her heart or her mouth.

Janie came back and put the plate on the counter in front of him. He looked up into her eyes, frantically listening, trying to hear.

"What is it, Sam?" she asked.

He shook his head. "Something's different."

"What?"

"I don't know." He got up and started backing out. "Uh, look. I can't eat right now." He threw a five-dollar bill down on the counter. "Maybe I'll come back in a little bit."

She nodded with confusion, and he bolted out of the diner and onto the sidewalk. A group of Girl Scouts passed by with boxes of cookies. Out here, when people passed him, he used to hear souls crying out their deepest needs. Now he heard nothing except the sounds of car engines going by, an occasional horn, voices from people chattering as they passed. But not the needs. Not those deep needs that stirred his heart.

Almost frantic with the fear that the gift was gone, he went to his car and drove to the bus station. There he would be able to tell if he had really lost his gift, he thought. There, where needs ran rampant and people were in turmoil. In the middle of a crowd, he would be able to tell.

He got there just as a bus was pulling in to let people out. It had been driving all night, he supposed, and the people were tired. They looked rumpled and wrinkled as they disembarked. He bypassed the terminal and headed straight for the bus. One by one the passengers got off, and he tried to hear.

But there was nothing. The gift was gone.

Tears burst into his eyes, and suddenly, he felt helpless, insignificant. Useless.

He ran back to his car. Where he would go, he wasn't sure, but he had to do something, he thought. John, his pastor, came to mind as he had on that first day. If anyone could help him, John could. So Sam pulled out and headed to John's home.

14

JOHN WAS SITTING AT HIS DESK IN HIS STUDY, HUNCHED over his Bible, when his wife let Sam in. Sam was as shaken as he'd been that first morning. He was drenched in sweat, breathing hard, and pushing trembling hands through his hair. "John, you've got to help me."

John looked alarmed. "Sam, are you okay?"

"It's gone!" he cried. "It's all gone!"

"What is?"

"The gift."

John got slowly to his feet. "How do you know?"

"I had another dream last night," Sam ranted. "When I woke up, I felt like something was different, and when I went to the diner, I couldn't hear the voices. I can't hear them anywhere, even at the bus station."

John's face went slack, and Sam realized how much of his hopes John had been pinning on Sam's gift. "Maybe it's just fading," John said. "Maybe it'll come back."

"No." Sam sat down and shook his head. "I just know

that it's gone. I think I knew on some level when I woke up this morning. After that dream . . ."

John took the seat next to him and leaned forward with his elbows on his knees. "Tell me about that dream," he said. "Sam, what happened in this one?"

"It was about the lost coin again," he said. "This time it was *my* coin, and I was looking instead of just watching someone else look. And then God spoke to me."

"What did he say this time?"

Sam hadn't thought about it since he'd told Kate earlier. He closed his eyes and tried to remember. "He said, 'And lo, I am with you always, even unto the end of the age.'"

John sat back in his chair. "That's the last verse in the Gospel of Matthew. The last words Matthew recorded before Jesus ascended."

"Why would he say that to me?" Sam asked. "What does it mean?"

"Just what it says, I'd imagine." He stared at Sam for a long moment. "Sam, are you sure it's gone?"

"Gone," he said. "I've tried. I can't hear a thing. Just normal voices. Just what you hear."

He saw that John was struggling to hide the disappointment on his face. "I had kind of counted on it staying. I mean, I don't know what I was thinking," John said. "Guess I was exploiting you in some ways."

"That was fine," Sam said. "After I got a taste of it, I *wanted* to be exploited. God gave me the gift for a reason."

John walked wearily back around his desk and dropped into his chair. "I really don't know what to think, Sam. Sometimes when I'm at a loss, the best thing to do is pray. Let's pray."

Sam gratefully hunched over, and as they began to pray, he felt a sadness fall over him. He knew with a certainty that the gift would not return. The Lord had given it, and he had taken it away. When they'd said "amen," John looked up at him, thoughts passing like shadows through his own eyes.

"Maybe the gift was just for a season, Sam. Let's not look at the removal of it as something to grieve about. Let's remember the joy while you had it. Maybe it was just to give you a glimpse of the urgency of the harvest."

"Maybe so," Sam said. "But it doesn't make it any easier." His mouth twisted as he tried not to cry, and he covered his face. "I was getting used to winning people to Christ. The confidence I had when I could just walk up to someone and know what their needs were. Hear inside them, just like the Lord does. What am I gonna do now?"

"You don't have to quit," John said. "You can still tell people about Jesus, just the way I do, and everybody else you taught does."

"No," Sam said. "I can't do it without that gift."

John got up, came closer, and touched Sam's shoulder.

"Go home and pray some more about this," he said. "Ask the Lord to show you what to do. He will. That's what his words were about, Sam. He hasn't left you. He's going to be right there with you."

But as Sam headed back out to his car, he felt very much alone.

15

S AM DIDN'T MAKE ANY STOPS ON THE WAY HOME. HE pulled into the garage and quickly closed the door behind him, as if it could keep him from having to encounter anyone whose needs he couldn't hear. He went into the house and saw that Kate was up and dressed. She smiled hopefully at him.

"Where ya been?"

"I just went to the diner to eat," he said.

She grinned. "How many?"

Tears sprang to his eyes, and he shook his head and headed toward the living room where he dropped into his recliner. Kate followed, the smile on her face fading. "What's the matter, Sam?"

"It's gone," he said. "I can't do it anymore."

"Do what?"

"I can't hear," he said. "The gift is all gone. I went everywhere. I went to the diner; I went out on the street; I went to the bus station. I can't hear it anymore!"

Kate stood there a moment, dumbfounded. Then, frowning, she asked, "Didn't you say you had a dream last night?"

"Yes," he said. "It must have been God's way of telling me it was over."

"Wow." She sank down onto the couch. "So . . . what are you gonna do?"

"Nothing. What *can* I do? I'm useless."

She thought about that for a moment, then stood back up. "Wait a minute. *I'm* not useless, and I haven't been able to hear anybody's spiritual needs."

"That's true," he said, "but you knew what I could hear. We were a team—I gave you information. But I can't do it anymore."

"No," she said. "That was true of the first few, but after that I got a little more confident. You weren't involved in every single one. Some of them I talked to without you."

"But let's face it," he said. "We both had this false sense of security that I could read their thoughts and know what they were feeling."

The telephone rang, and Kate stared at Sam for a moment, obviously processing his words. He could see that she was going to protest again, but instead, she picked up the phone. "Hello? Yeah, he's here. Just a minute." She held the phone out to Sam. "It's Steve."

"I don't want to talk to him. I'm too strung out here."

"He already knows you're here," she whispered.

Sighing heavily, Sam grabbed the phone. "Hello."

"Sam, it's Steve. Listen, Joan and I went to the mall this morning, and there was this old man who'd been sitting on a bench all by himself, and I finally got up the nerve to approach him and start a conversation, and you're not gonna believe what happened."

"What?"

"He accepted Christ. He's gonna come to church in the morning."

Sam closed his eyes and smiled faintly. "That's good, Steve. That's great."

"And I was just wondering, if you're not doing anything, why don't you come on over here? I'm gonna be here for a while. There are people everywhere. I thought you and I could—"

"No," Sam cut in. "I can't."

"Oh." Steve sounded a little surprised. "Well, okay, that's fine, if you have another commitment."

Sam shook his head. "Not another commitment, Steve. It's not that. It's just that—" He glanced up at Kate. Their eyes locked. He knew she was waiting to see what he was going to tell him. "It's just that I'm not feeling very well. I kind of have a . . . an ear problem."

"That doesn't sound good. Well, don't worry about it, then. I'll just work on my courage. You know, I'm counting on having a 'Let Us Rejoice' party every Friday night."

Sam frowned. He couldn't see it happening. Not now, not without his gift. Things had changed.

"I'll just call Bill and Jeff and see if they want to come. They had a blast last night. It was like they suddenly dis-covered a talent they didn't know they had. Listen, you take care, okay? Hope you're feeling better by tomorrow."

Sam hung up the phone and stared at it for a moment.

"Steve asked you to go with him to tell people about Jesus, and you turned him down?"

"Kate, didn't you hear me? It's over!"

The doorbell rang, and Kate headed for it. Moments later, John was in the doorway. "He lost the gift," Kate was telling him, and John was nodding.

"I know. He came by the house and told me this morning."

Sam began to rub his temples, but John came farther into the room and sat down opposite him. "You won't believe this."

"Tell me," Sam said, not very enthusiastically.

John leaned his elbows on his knees. "I've been getting calls this morning from some of the people in the evangelism class. The party last night got them all excited, and they're starting to feel more confident. They want to go out and talk to people after class tomorrow afternoon. Bill and Steve and Jeff told me to sign them up last night. I just wanted to let you know. I thought that might cheer you up, since you started all this."

Sam shrugged. "I appreciate that. I guess the gift did a lot of good while it lasted."

"But it didn't do you any good, did it?" Kate asked.

Irritated, Sam looked up at his wife. "What is that supposed to mean?"

"You're just gonna quit, like you can't mention the name Jesus without some supernatural gift. But none of the rest of us have it, and we can do it. There's still a harvest, Sam."

"Hey, you didn't go out until I taught you how. Until I could feed you their thoughts."

"Well, I've done it *without* knowing their thoughts," she said. "I can do it again. I have the courage. Do you?"

John looked as if he'd gotten caught in the middle of a family squabble. Defeated, Sam sank back in his chair and said, "What do you want from me, John?"

"I just wanted to see if you would come to the class tomorrow. Go out with us. Help them get started."

"Why me?"

"Because God touched you, Sam. He had a reason. He blessed you with revelations that the rest of us haven't had. You know things. And people respect you because you've succeeded."

"Then how come I feel like a failure?"

"Because you're not looking at it with God's eyes."

Sam stayed home from church the next morning, and Kate went alone. He didn't have the energy or the desire to go.

But when she got back from church and told him that thirty-six people had professed Christ that day, he began to feel guilty for his attitude. "I'm going to the class this afternoon," Kate said. "I wish you would go with me."

He hadn't enjoyed spending Sunday morning in a dark living room, while his wife was worshiping without him. He knew he was being selfish. His brooding was only making him feel worse and was keeping him from the people who mattered most to him. "All right," he said. "I'll go with you. But I'm only doing it to show you that this is not going to work."

"It will work," Kate said. "That gift taught you how to care about people. And I don't think your compassion will disappear just because your radar isn't picking up their thoughts anymore." Her gaze softened as she touched his shoulders and looked into his eyes. "Tell me your compassion isn't gone, Sam. I liked being married to someone who cared."

Sam wanted to tell her that he was still that person, but he wasn't sure he was. Would his zeal cool to a lukewarm level as it had been before? Would his heart grow hard again?

He turned away. Behind him, he heard her heavy sigh. "It's up to you, Sam. You had a two-week crash course in being like Jesus. Are you gonna throw that back in God's face?"

A million answers shot through Sam's mind, but he wasn't sure of any of them. He turned around and stared helplessly at her.

"I know how crushed you must be," she said softly. "I'm

kind of crushed myself. But God has his reasons, Sam. You have to trust him."

"John wants me to keep being some kind of leader . . . to tell others how to win souls . . . to act like I know something they don't know. But I *don't*. Not anymore."

Kate's eyes brimmed with tears. "Sam, don't you care about the lost coin anymore? Doesn't it matter to you?"

Sam couldn't take the sting of her words. He went to the kitchen and grabbed his keys off of the counter. "I've got to think," he said. "I need to be alone. I'll just . . . meet you at the class."

"Will you really be there?" she asked, sounding as if she didn't carry much hope that he really would. "Do you promise?"

He hesitated for a long moment, searching her face for the answers he couldn't find within himself. "I promise."

Then, before she could probe deeper, he hurried to the car.

Sam drove around town for several hours, thinking and praying about the things that had happened to him. For the life of him, he couldn't understand the Lord's playing such a cruel trick on him. Why would he have thrust an unwanted gift on him, then taught him to cherish it, only to take it away? It didn't make sense.

He pulled up next to a park where children played, and he began to walk the path that wound through the trees. He found a bench in the shade and sat down as joggers ran by, their sneakers thudding on the concrete. On the playground just beyond the running path, children laughed and squealed, and dogs barked.

There was so much to hear, yet so little. It was all superficial now. He might as well be deaf.

He checked his watch and saw that it was time to head to the church. He had promised Kate, and he didn't like to break promises. He wondered if the class members would be able to see right through him. Wouldn't they know that something inside him had been snatched away? That he didn't have the "insights" anymore?

I want to hear like you do, Lord. I want to know what you know.

But as he ambled back to his car, he felt the hopeless, sick feeling that he would never come close to hearing like that again.

16

S AM WAS STUNNED WHEN HE WALKED INTO THE classroom that afternoon and saw the number of people who had come to learn how to share their faith. He looked around and guessed that there were at least a hundred people there. Some baby Christians, some who'd been believers for years. Bill and Steve were bringing in extra chairs, and Sam joined in. At least he could do that, he thought.

When John finally got the class quiet, he searched the room. "Sam, would you come up here for a minute, please?"

Sam shot John a look that told him he was going too far. He set down the chairs he was carrying and moved to the front of the room.

"Sam, everybody here knows the success rate you've had in telling people about Christ," John said. "It's inspired all of us. Now, you can see from the size of this class, the fruit that it's borne. And I wanted you to stand up here for a minute and tell people what your secret is."

Shocked, Sam gaped at his pastor. Why would John

humiliate him like this? What did he expect him to say? That he'd had a supernatural gift of hearing peoples' souls? John stepped closer and lowered his voice. "Sam, tell them what to do. Tell them how to listen. Tell them what to see. You know."

Sam's eyes filled with tears, and his mouth trembled as he shifted from one foot to the other. He met Kate's hopeful eyes, and she nodded for him to answer. He cleared his throat and tried to speak. His voice cracked as it came out. "Well, basically, the bottom line, I guess, is . . ." He cleared it again. "Well, uh . . . you just . . . listen. Listen to them talk. Look at their faces. Look in their eyes. Touch them. Use your common sense." Yes, he thought. That was exactly what he had done every time he'd had any success. Something inside him stirred, and he took a step toward the class.

"If you could just hear with the ears of God, for a day, or a week, or two weeks . . ." He wiped the tears before they could run down his face. "If you could hear what God hears, you'd never forget it." He stopped and took a deep breath and met Kate's eyes, then John's. "There's not a soul out there who doesn't have those spiritual needs. You've got to learn to look for them."

Someone in the back of the room raised her hand, and he nodded for her to speak. "Sam, what would you say is their most common spiritual need?"

He shrugged and thought the question over for a long

moment, juggling the different answers that came to him, try-ing to decide what the most common and most important ones were. "Well, they need to know that they're loved, that there's hope, that there's healing, that someone's in control, that they're not a product of their past, that they can be for-given, that they can be useful, that they're made in the image of God . . ." He paused and racked his brain for more.

But suddenly it came to him. There really was only one answer that filled those needs he'd been naming. The answer he'd been offering for the past two weeks.

He stood there for a moment as the thought took hold of him. "You know, really," he said, "I guess the answer to all their questions, the fulfillment of all of their needs, is Jesus Christ."

They were hanging on every word, and he looked around at them as the thought sank deeper. "Really," he said. "Anybody you walked up to, if you were to ask them what their deepest need was, and if they were to be perfectly hon-est, if they even knew . . . their answer would be Jesus Christ."

He glanced awkwardly at the pastor and saw that John was grinning.

Encouraged, Sam went on, "So what we need to do is go out there with the knowledge that we have information they don't have. We can tell them how to fulfill those needs. We can turn their lives around. They all have the same need, and that need is Jesus Christ."

"What if they already know Jesus?" someone else asked. "What would their need be then?"

Sam looked from his wife to his friends, to the people he had led to Christ. And then he knew.

I want a broken heart.

I need to be used.

I've wasted all those years.

He covered his mouth as those tears erupted again. Finally, he managed to speak, "The bottom-line, basic need of every real Christian," he said, "is to bear fruit like Christ. You can count on it. Every true Christian has that need, whether they want to admit it or not. The Holy Spirit in them, it just yearns for that. And the further they are from fulfilling it, the emptier they are. Jesus cares about filling that emptiness . . . for a lot of reasons. One of them is our own happiness, but the bigger reason is that . . . it's not about us. It's about advancing God's kingdom. *We're* about advancing God's kingdom. And if we aren't acting like Christ, then we're missing it. It's like we're children of the king, but we're living in a dirt shack and eating pig food."

He saw in their faces that they all understood. He saw the glow of excitement in their eyes, the tears of resolve and commitment.

"Once you start behaving like Christ, in every area of your life, it's like moving into the castle," Sam said. "You know you don't deserve that joy, but it's still yours. You are who you are. You have power and the inheritance and all the joy that comes with it. And once you feel that joy . . ." His voice broke off, and he looked down at his feet and struggled to rein in his emotions. "Once you have it, you'll never want to be without it again."

After the class, John suggested that they all go out somewhere and practice sharing their faith before their zeal started to fade. Sam felt that fear he'd had in the beginning, the first day he'd realized he had the gift. But as the people began getting their bags and coats and heading for the church vans, he realized that he had to do better than this. He couldn't be a coward. He knew more than they knew. He had been enlightened. And tonight, the truth had come from his very own lips. The further he was from being like Christ, the more unhappy he would be. He knew it firsthand. How could he go back now?

John patted him on the back as they left the room. "So where do you think we ought to go?" he asked.

Sam thought for a moment. "Let's go to the bus station," he said. "There's a bus due in about ten minutes. And those people need the Lord."

17

NEEDING TO BE ALONE, SAM TOOK HIS OWN CAR AND
followed behind the vans to the station. As he drove,
he felt a sinking feeling in the pit of his stomach. What
would they say when they saw what a failure he was? Would
they all quit? Would they laugh at him?

The vans parked, and his church friends began filing out
just as a bus pulled up. He sat in his car for a moment as the
weary travelers began to get off the bus. His eyes burned with
fear, and his heart pounded. As he got out, he breathed a silent
prayer, a prayer for courage, a prayer for confidence, a prayer
that he could hear as the Holy Spirit heard.

The group of them broke up, and each approached
someone and struck up a conversation. Sam stood with his
hands in his pockets and listened as he heard various ones
around the room explaining Christ in the best way they
knew how. He saw an older man standing near the glass doors,
looking out as if waiting for someone to pick him up. But
no one ever came. Sam looked around, helplessly wondering

whom he should approach, what he should say to them when he couldn't confidently know what their needs were. Then he remembered the theory he'd come to in the classroom a little earlier . . . that every lost soul's need was the same.

Deciding to approach the man under that premise, he went to the door. "Hey, there," he said as he reached him. "How ya doing?"

The man nodded and smiled weakly.

"My name's Sam Bennett," he said, reaching out to shake his hand. "You waiting for somebody?"

"I thought I was," the rumpled old man said. "I thought my daughter was coming to get me, but—" His eyes reddened with emotion, and he looked away. "We don't get along so well and . . . I didn't really know if she'd come or not."

Sam's heart began to melt, and he realized that he was hearing the need. He looked through the glass door in the direction where the man had been looking. "Maybe she'll still come," he said. "Maybe she's just late."

The old man's mouth trembled as he shook his head. "No, I don't think she's gonna come. See, it's been a long time since I've been in touch with her, and well . . . I guess I crossed over the point where there's no goin' back."

Sam met his eyes and remembered the lost things of Luke 15. The lost coin . . . the lost sheep . . . the lost son. The poignancy of those stories assaulted him anew, and he realized that the Holy Spirit had reminded him so that he could tell the man. "There's never a point where you've gone too far," he said.

The man breathed in a heavy, soul-deep sigh. "Oh, yeah there is. And I crossed it a long time ago." Sam looked out the door again, wishing the daughter would come to show the man that there was such a thing as forgiveness and new life. But even if she didn't, there was someone else who would. There was a father, scanning the horizon for the sight of that lost son. "Why don't you let me give you a ride?" Sam asked. "I have my car out here."

"Weren't you waiting for somebody else?"

Sam shrugged. "Sort of. But they didn't show up either." The man looked at Sam with new eyes, as if he could understand how it felt to be rejected. "Come on. I'll take you to wherever you need to go."

"Well, I appreciate that, sir," the man said. "Don't you need to tell your friends?"

Sam looked over toward Kate. She was watching him and smiling. He winked and nodded that he was leaving. "It's okay," he said. "They've got another way home."

As he got into the car with the old man and asked where he wanted to go, he realized that the needs were right there on the surface . . . in the man's face . . . in his stance . . . in the way he carried himself . . . in his words. And what he couldn't hear, the Holy Spirit could. He could do what Sam couldn't.

This man needed Jesus Christ.

That was all he needed to know.

Reading Group Guide

Read the three parables in Luke 15. What was Jesus trying to show in these parables? If you could sum them up in one sentence, what would it be?

1. How do these parables relate to you?

2. If you are a Christian, how should you respond to these parables?

3. Read Ezekiel 3. What does this passage mean to you?

4. Even though we can't hear the voices of souls crying out, what are some ways we can understand people's needs?

5. Think of times you've missed opportunities to share Christ with others. What could you have

done differently? Rehearse those conversations the way you wish they had gone so you'll be prepared the next time an opportunity arises.

6. Look up Acts 4:18-20. Do you feel the way Peter and John do about telling people about Christ?

7. Think about the people with whom you've come into contact in the last few days. What needs might they have had? Did the Holy Spirit give you any impressions of those people?

8. Rehearse a conversation in which you might have met their needs.

9. Why are some Christians (you? me?) so reluctant to share their faith?

10. Read the Great Commission, Matthew 28: 19–20. How important were Christ's last words before ascending to heaven?

11. What do you think Jesus meant when he said, "And lo, I will be with you, even unto the end of the age"?

12. What do you think is everyone's deepest need? Are you able to fill that need?

13. Even though you don't have the gift of hearing the voices of people's souls, how has the Holy Spirit gifted you to meet their needs?

14. Read Romans 10:14 and 15. Do you have beautiful feet?

15. Pray for God to give you the courage and the words to take His good news to a hurting world.

the Gifted

This book is lovingly dedicated to the Nazarene.

INTRODUCTION

YEARS AGO, WHEN I WAS A DIVORCED MOTHER
of two little girls looking for a church home, I went
from church to church, desperately seeking a place where
I felt accepted rather than shunned—a place where I
could grow in Christ and get my life back on track. Thankfully, the Lord led me to that place, and that was the
beginning of my healing . . . and my journey back to
God.

Some time later, as my pastor spoke to the congregation about our mission to help hurting people, he said that
Christians too often shoot their wounded. He said that
our church's mission was "to send an ambulance instead of
a firing squad." And that's just what that church did for
me, through people who'd experienced what I was suffering, and others who used their God-given gifts to minister to me in my time of need.

But I don't see that working in every church, nor do I

see it working in my own all the time. Too often, I see five percent of the congregation doing a hundred percent of the work. The other ninety-five percent just wants to be fed. They sit in their pews Sunday after Sunday, like the man-eating plant in "Little Shop of Horrors" crying, "Feed Me, Seymour!" And the workers do everything they can to accommodate.

That's why I wanted to write *The Gifted.* I wanted to show what could happen if we each used our gifts as God intended. What might that look like in the church? And how would it change us to see God working through those gifts, using every part of the Body of Christ, to minister to a hurting world?

It's my prayer that this book will make readers think about the ways they've been gifted, and prompt them to ask themselves how God might have intended to use those special, unique gifts. Sometimes that gifting takes the form of a talent or skilled service, which God honed in them for a specific purpose. Sometimes it takes the form of an affliction, or an experience of tragedy or suffering, which can be used to help others stuck in the depths of despair. Sometimes it's service or compassion . . . gifts we think aren't important. But God knows they are, and He had a plan for them when He gave them to us.

As you read this book, keep your own gifts in mind. When you're finished, allow the study questions at the end to help you prayerfully seek God's will in your life.

Then imagine the Body of Christ with no paralyzed members, actively laboring in the fields that are ripe for harvest!

1

T HIS JUST ISN'T WORKING." BREE HARRIS CLOSED
her Bible and looked at her co-workers across the
table. Andy Hendrix and Carl Dennis looked as frustrated
as she. "I thought you said this Bible study was going to be
an outreach, that we were going to talk it up and get half
the office studying with us every Thursday. That was the
plan, wasn't it?"

"I thought *you* said you were going to be the one to
print out the fliers, telling people about it." Carl Dennis
looked disgusted as he got up and crossed the employees'
lounge. The office coffeepot was filled to capacity, even
though there were only three of them here. "Where are
those brochures?" he asked as he poured himself a cup. "I
never saw them."

"I was busy, okay? I didn't have time. You could have
done them, you know."

Andy sat slumped at the table, his Bible open in front of him. "Bree, you're supposed to be the big desktop-publishing whiz. When we talked about this at church, you said it would be easy. You were even excited about it."

"I know." Bree groaned out the words. "I blew it, okay? I should have done it, but I didn't."

"It's okay." Andy left his Bible on the table and joined Carl at the coffee. "We don't have to have a bunch of people in this. We can do it with just us."

The two men made an amusing picture standing side by side. Andy was six feet four and three hundred pounds; Carl was only five-five and probably weighed 130 pounds soaking wet. But their personalities didn't match their statures. Carl said whatever came to his mind—good or bad—as if he didn't realize that almost anyone in the office could pin him to the floor in the time it took to call him a jerk. Though Andy looked a lot like one of those cocky television wrestlers who ranted and raved threats, he was mild mannered and quiet.

"I know we can do it with just us," Bree said, "but having the Bible study was supposed to be for a purpose. A way to share Christ with our coworkers. I just don't get it. Half the people up here claim to be Christians, but when we start a once-a-week Bible study for thirty stinking minutes after work, nobody has time for it. It kind of makes me mad, you know? I mean, what are the unbelievers supposed to think?"

"Like I said," Carl piped in, "they're not going to think *anything* because they weren't even aware we were having it."

Bree bristled. "Hey, I did put it in last week's newsletter. I also sent an e-mail around to everybody."

Carl sipped his coffee. "Nobody reads those things. I get a million e-mails a day. I delete half of them."

"I also invited a lot of people personally. That should have carried more weight than anything else."

"I did too." Carl sat back down. "I told everybody I've seen for the last three days, and I heard excuses that would singe your hair."

"Well, *we're* here." Andy came back to the table and set his coffee down. "We can do this. I've been working on my lesson all week."

To Bree, that was the biggest problem. When the idea had come up to start this Bible study where they worked, Andy had quickly volunteered to teach it. In her opinion, he was the worst choice. His soft, level monotone would probably put them right to sleep. It was clear that he was following their pastor's admonition to step out of his comfort zone, but she wished they didn't all have to pay for his growth.

She just didn't have the heart to say so. "Okay, Andy. You've got the floor."

Carl came and sat down, but the look on his face said that his thoughts mirrored Bree's.

Andy cleared his throat twice, sipped his coffee, then pulled his notes out of his Bible. "Maybe we could open with a prayer?"

Bree glanced at Carl. "All right."

Andy took both of their hands and bowed his head.

A rumbling sounded over the building, and the coffee in Carl's cup began to slosh. The framed "Character First" sign hanging on the wall crashed to the floor.

Andy's grip on their hands tightened slightly. "It's just a tremor."

But it was more than a tremor. Other pictures fell, and the chairs they sat in began to vibrate and move beneath them. The coffeepot jerked its way across the counter and crashed onto the floor.

Carl jumped up. "Earthquake! Get into a doorway!"

"Not a doorway," Bree cried. "We'll never make it. Get under the table!"

The three of them dove under the table as the

rumbling grew louder. The floor began to crumble, and Bree had the terrifying sensation of hunkering over unsupported plaster that was falling apart beneath her. She screamed.

Plaster from the ceiling began to snow down on them. "The ceiling!" she cried. "We have to get out."

She tried to crawl toward the door, but Andy pulled her back. "The wall's coming down! Cover yourself!"

She got back under the table and covered her head as the wall collapsed on itself, making the rest of the room slant and splinter like a house made of toothpicks. The floor beneath them tilted to one side, rumbling like waves, and the table started to slide.

Bree shrieked out her horror as she began to slide down the incline of the floor. The three-story building above them came down in slow motion, walls crashing, the ceiling caving, people yelling above them.

The light blacked out, and all went dark, but the rumbling didn't stop. The building continued falling on top of them, burying them alive.

2

WHEN THE RUMBLING AND CRUMBLING STOPPED, Bree forced herself to think beyond the panic gripping her. Her body felt bruised, but she didn't think anything was broken. She tried to force her arms through the plaster and concrete pinning her to the rubble beneath her.

"Andy? Carl? Where are you?"

"I'm here." It was Carl's voice.

Relief flooded through her. "Andy?"

Andy spoke up. "I'm here, but I can't move. Something's crushing me."

"Me too," Carl said. "I'm pinned down. Man, three floors fell on top of us. How are we still alive?"

"I don't know." Bree wondered how deeply they were buried. "Maybe we'd better not try to move too much. We might start another avalanche."

They lay silent for a moment, listening for the sounds that might foretell another tremor.

"It was a bad one," Bree said finally.

Andy agreed. "Had to be eight or nine on the Richter scale. We're probably not the only building in town that's fallen."

Bree didn't want to hear that. She pictured the whole town devastated—bridges collapsed, streets buckled, homes and schools destroyed. She thought of her children. Her mother had picked them up from school. They were at home with her by now. Had they been buried too?

Rescue workers were probably combing the streets, looking for victims even now. What if there were so many that it took them days to work their way here?

Horror caught in her throat as she pictured her children buried just like this, unable to help themselves. She imagined seven-year-old Amy's terrified screams and eight-year-old Brad's desperate attempts to dig his way out. *Please God, save my kids!* "Thank goodness it happened after work," Carl said. "There probably weren't many people left in the building."

Andy moaned. "Man, I wasn't even supposed to *be* here today."

Bree tried to concentrate on the sound of his voice. If she could keep her mind focused somewhere else, she might be able to hold the panic at bay. "Where were you supposed to be?"

"I had a doctor's appointment. I was supposed to get a physical, but then I remembered that I was teaching the Bible study so I postponed it. Pretty weird, huh?"

The rumbling started again, and Bree groped for something to hold on to. She screamed as the rubble beneath her shifted and rolled. She felt a hand . . . and grabbed onto it.

"I've got you," Carl shouted. "Andy, grab my hand! Grab it, Andy!"

A cruel roar sounded around them, and Bree heard things collapsing, crashing, falling . . . She felt the impact as debris caved down onto the table pinning them down. She twisted her head sideways and felt as if her neck would pop or her jaw would collapse as the table legs had done. The concrete block wall next to them crumbled and buried their legs. They all screamed out.

Bree began to pray as loud and as hard as she could, pleading with God to spare her, her children, and Andy and Carl.

Then the floor fell out from under her again, and she heard a small explosion and the sound of shattering glass. It sprayed into her eyes, tiny shards of metal and glass, cutting into her corneas and the skin of her face.

It was as though someone had taken an ice pick and made a sieve out of her eyes. She screamed out, but couldn't even get her hands to her face.

Darkness fell over her, and she knew she'd been blinded. If she survived this earthquake at all, she would likely never see again.

⸺⸺

Carl fell with the floor, praying that he would hit bottom soon and that the weight of the building would shift and avoid crushing them. Something jagged broke his fall, but his back buckled in pain. He wiggled to move off of whatever lay beneath him, but a steel beam crashed across his legs, pinning him.

Pain shot through him like an internal fireworks display, racking his nerves and stretching his tendons, cracking his vertebrae and crushing his legs.

His screams echoed through his own head, reverberated through the devastated room, and competed with the sounds of the screams he heard next to him.

⸺⸺

At first all was dark, then Andy saw the flicker of bright orange dancing through the mounds of rubble that lay next to him. He tried to move toward it, figuring that light must provide some means of escape. But then he felt its heat.

"Something's burning!" He fought to move away, but couldn't. "Fire!"

"We're gonna die!" Bree's cry sounded as though she was still close by.

Carl moaned. "Where's the fire? I don't smell anything."

"It's where I am." Andy choked on the smoke as it filled his air hole. He coughed and tried to turn his head, but he couldn't move. "Help!"

Hot, searing smoke whispered around him to the background song of the crackling fire. He tried not to breathe, but he could only hold his breath so long. Finally, he gasped in air, and scalding smoke shot down his throat, blistering everything in its path, searing his vocal cords, and trapping itself in his lungs.

He coughed and sputtered, but it felt as if the flames were licking his throat, taunting him, destroying him in some slow, evil way. He tried to speak, but his throat felt bloody and ruined.

"Andy, are you all right?" Carl's voice wavered on the edge of panic. "Where's the fire?"

He coughed again, trying to force the smoke out of his lungs, but there was more behind it, growing hotter and more deadly.

"Andy!" Carl's voice was strained and tight. "Andy, move toward me. I'm not getting the smoke. There's clear air toward me."

Andy tried to squirm toward Carl's voice. With all his strength, he managed to turn his body away from the flames and dug through the pieces of concrete next to him.

"I can't move my legs," Carl said. "They're crushed. But I can move my arms. I'll try to dig through to you."

Andy heard scraping next to him, and he tried to match it. Behind him, the rubble shifted again. He dug with his hands toward the sound of Carl's voice until finally he reached the steel beam holding Carl in place. He touched Carl's belt.

Carl's hand grabbed his, and clung for dear life.

"You're okay, Andy. Just get in here where you can breathe."

Behind him, Andy heard more debris moving, falling . . .

The heat of the fire cooled at his back. Maybe the fire had been smothered. He snaked his way through the rubble until he finally gasped a breath of fresh air. "I'm here." His voice was a pitiful squeal. "Fire's out."

"Thank you, God." Carl's hand trembled. "Bree, where are you?"

"To your left, Carl." Her voice was a high squeal. "But I can't see. Glass or metal or something shattered into my eyes."

Andy winced. It was hard to know whose injury was more severe. His throat still felt as if he'd swallowed hot coals, and from the size of the beam across Carl's legs, he was sure that Carl's legs were crushed. And now Bree's blindness . . .

"Try to reach toward me," Carl said. "Grab my hand."

Andy heard scraping again, shifting rubble, grunting . . .

"I've got you!" Carl's voice broke. "We're all together now. We're okay. Let's not let each other go. We'll get through this together."

Bree began to cry, deep, panicked sobs. "My children . . ."

"Let's pray," Carl said. "Come on, Bree. Calm down, and let's pray."

Bree grew quiet, and Carl began to lift up their pain

and fear and panic to the only One who knew for sure what their future held.

When they finished praying through the anguish of their pain and terror, they lay clutching each other's hands, waiting.

"I don't even have a will prepared." Bree hated the eerie way her voice echoed in the silence. "I don't know who will take care of my children. They're so young. They need me."

"We can't give up." Carl's voice rose in pitch, as if he spoke through soul-splitting pain. "We have to get out of here."

Bree tried to push up with her body, but it was no use. "There must be something we can do. Make noise or something. Maybe they're out there looking for us."

"Maybe she's got a point." Carl's trembling hand tightened on Bree's. "Maybe we need to make some noise, keep talking so that if they have any of those ultrasensitive microphones they'll pick us up. We could sing."

"Sing?" Bree couldn't stand the thought. "Are you out of your mind?"

"A hymn," he said. "The Bible says we should praise God in all things. If we need to make noise, singing would do it."

"I know we're supposed to praise Him," Bree said, "but I think He understands if we don't feel like singing now."

"Fine. Then talk, and keep talking until someone finds us."

The pain in Bree's eyes distracted her, and she couldn't think of what to say. So she talked about that. "My eyes feel like a dozen ice picks are stabbing through them. Even if we live, I may never see again—" Her voice broke, and she felt that panic rising again. She drew a deep, calming breath and forced herself to go on. "I don't want to be blind. I want to see my children's faces again. I want another chance to appreciate how beautiful they are. I never appreciate anything! Rainbows, sunsets, snow-peaked mountains . . . I've taken them all for granted. And people . . . I go around looking right through them, never really seeing them . . ."

She let her voice trail off, then finally whispered, "Go ahead and sing. My rambling isn't doing us any good."

Carl cleared his throat. She had heard him sing in church, and he was basically as tone deaf as they come. But that didn't matter now.

He began to sing the chorus to "We Are Standing on Holy Ground," and when he came to the part about angels standing all around, Bree cut in.

"Do you think there are? Angels, I mean."

"If God ever uses angels, and we know He does, I'll bet He's using them now."

Carl kept singing, and finally Bree joined in. The simple song got her mind off of the pain in her caked, bloody eyes, and calmed her panicked spirit.

———

Carl formed the groans in his throat into the words of the song, trying to concentrate on the angels of God hovering around them rather than the angel of death that surely loomed over them. But the pain twisted through his body, making him want to scream.

Wasn't that a good sign? Pain might mean that he wasn't paralyzed. If his spinal cord was damaged, wouldn't he be numb?

He sang on, trying to think of the pain as a good thing, but he couldn't escape the picture of himself in a wheelchair, never able to walk again.

Then he thought of all those nights he'd spent propped up in his recliner watching football on ESPN. Nights he could have been out pounding the pavement to tell people about Christ.

If he was to meet God soon, what would He say about

that? *Wasted a lot of time, didn't you, son? I gave you two perfectly good legs. Why you kept them propped up all the time as though you were recovering from surgery is beyond Me.*

Carl's response would probably be as lame as the earthquake had left him. "I worked hard all day, Lord. I thought it would be okay if I just chilled for a while."

He closed his eyes against the regret. *God, please, give me a chance to clean up my heart, even if I can never use my legs again.* He wasn't ready to face the throne of God just yet. There were too many things he had to do—if he ever got out of this place.

He kept singing, forcing himself to be as loud as the pain was intense, praying that someone above all the rubble would hear.

Andy wanted to join in, but his vocal chords felt as if they had melted in the searing smoke. He couldn't make a sound come from his throat.

Even if a miracle occurred and they did survive this live burial, would he ever be able to speak again? He closed his eyes, mentally singing with his friends, trying to make the soft, sweet tune calm him and dull his pain.

What if his vocal chords were ruined, and he could

never utter a word again? What if he never got the chance to say all those things he'd put off saying? There were so many people out there he'd meant to tell about Christ, but he'd hardly ever opened his mouth to tell of his Savior—

He grimaced. What was he thinking? It was probably too late. He probably wouldn't live to tell anyone anything.

When Bree and Carl reached the end of the song, Bree spoke first. "I've always wondered what people feel like when they know they're going to die and leave their children behind. How they manage to trust God to take care of them."

"He will, you know." Carl's voice held a note of determination. "He'll take care of them."

"But they can't go live with their dad. He's not fit to take care of them, and my mother's not capable of doing it alone. She doesn't have much money, and her health isn't good. My sister's got a career. It would just disrupt her lifestyle too much to have two kids in the house."

Andy could hear the despair in her voice. For the first time in a long time, he was glad he didn't have a wife or kids to leave behind.

Bree went on. "I shouldn't have spoiled them so. I shouldn't have spent so much time with them, because now it'll hurt them so for me to be gone. I shouldn't have read them stories at night before they went to bed, or snuggled them up in their beds, or laid down with them until they went to sleep."

"How can you *say* that?" Carl choked the words out. "Bree, those are good things. You shouldn't regret those."

"But I should have prepared them."

"How do you prepare a child for something like this? You can't. You just do the best you can while you're there." Tears filled Andy's eyes at Bree's plight, and for Carl's . . . and for his.

They sang again, one song after another, and Andy locked in on the words assuring him of God's mighty sovereignty, of His goodness and mercy, of His presence in times of distress.

Finally, they prayed again.

"Lord—" Bree's voice was so low that Andy almost couldn't hear—"Lord, if You'll get me out of here, I'll do better, I promise. I won't take so much for granted, and I'll use my time better. I'll devote my life to serving You. Please, won't You give me another chance?"

Silence passed, and they waited. Andy wondered why

they heard nothing above them. No sirens, no digging, no voices calling out.

"At least we all know we're going to heaven if we die." Carl's voice wavered with each word. "We don't have to be afraid."

Andy heard the sound of Bree sobbing. "I'm not afraid for me," she said. "I'm afraid for my kids. I know I'm supposed to trust. I know that whatever God has in store for them, it's right and it's good. And I know He'll take care of them if He takes me out of this life. I even know that maybe He needs for them to go through this to become the people He wants them to be." Her voice broke off. More crying. He wished he could reach her and comfort her in some way.

"I've said that to other people who were dying," Bree went on. "I've written it in condolence cards. And I believe it now . . . but I can't help thinking it would be so much better if it didn't have to happen.

"I'm sorry, Lord." Bree spoke as if He lay there among them, holding her hand with the others. "I know we're supposed to be excited about seeing You. Coming home is supposed to be such a joyful event. It's just that I always pictured it being different, like at the end of my life . . . when I could look back and know that I'd done everything I was supposed to do. I can't do that right now."

Andy squeezed his eyes shut, echoing her prayer. *Me too Lord. I'm sorry too.* Carl started to sing again. Bree began to sing along.

Something shifted, and powder blew down on Andy's face. He squeezed Carl's hand, shutting him up.

"Shhh," Carl told Bree. "I hear something."

Bree got quiet and listened.

Something moved above them. "Do you think it's starting again?" Bree asked. "Another aftershock?"

"No," Carl said. "It's somebody digging! We've got to yell. Everybody yell. Help! Help us! Can you hear us?"

They heard a voice then, and Bree started laughing, a pained, hysterical, gushing relief kind of laughter.

"We're coming for you," the voice called. "Just hold tight."

Andy had heard accounts of near-death experiences, where the dead had seen a white light at the end of a dark tunnel, beckoning them toward the afterlife. When light broke through the darkness of the destruction around him, he knew it meant life for him too. He felt the brisk, fresh air blowing through the hole . . . and his lungs rebelled in a fit of coughing.

"How many of you are down there?"

"Three," Carl yelled up, then the digging got louder and more urgent, and Andy felt the weight of the concrete being lifted off of him, felt steel and bricks falling away.

"We got 'em!" somebody shouted.

Andy heard them working near Bree, scraping and yelling and pulling . . . and finally he heard her voice lifting over his head as they pulled her into the light.

"See about her eyes!" one of the rescuers yelled to the others.

"Get the others out," Andy heard Bree say. "Andy had smoke inhalation and can't breathe or talk. And Carl is crushed. Please get them out!"

He saw them coming back into the tunnel and heard power tools start up. When the buzzing died, someone yelled, "We've got to get Carl first before we can get to Andy. Are both of you all right?"

Carl spoke up. "Andy can't answer. He breathed in a lot of smoke. He's having trouble breathing. He wants you to hurry."

Andy smiled. *Carl, you read my mind.*

It took a few minutes for them to cut Carl out of his vise, but when they got him on the gurney, Andy knew he was going to have to let go of his hand.

He dreaded letting go. Panic sweated over him as he opened his fingers and felt his friend slipping away. What if they got Carl out and the rubble shifted again, this time crushing him? What if the tunnel they'd dug closed up and they couldn't get him out?

His heart hammered out its impatience as he waited for them to come back for him. Then he saw them hurrying back into the hole, and they reached him and pulled him out. It was like sliding through a birth canal, into the light of life. As he came into the day, he felt the jolt of that rebirth, into a world that seemed to have gone haywire.

3

PARAMEDICS SCURRIED AROUND BREE, CHECKING her eyes and sticking a needle into her arm. She could hear rescue workers yelling, television reporters doing live coverage, bystanders chattering and crying.

But she couldn't make out light or shapes, shadows or grays. All was black.

Still, that wasn't the main thing on her mind. "My children! I need to call—"

"Ma'am, we've got to get you to the hospital as soon as possible."

"But if I could just use a cell phone—"

"All the lines are jammed since the quake."

It must have been bad. Horrible. There were probably people buried all over the city. Brad . . . Amy . . .

They loaded her into the ambulance and closed the doors, shutting out the noise. *I'm alive.* She ran that

thought through her mind again and again, focusing on
the gratitude she felt rather than the paralyzing fear for
her children, her mother, her eyes . . .

They reached the hospital in no time, and she jumped
as the ambulance doors burst open. Her gurney was jerked
out, and she had the strange sense of falling as they raced
with her gurney toward some unseen target.

She heard crying and wailing around her, doctors
calling out orders, nurses talking loudly to other patients.

"Glass and metal fragments in the eyes," someone
beside her yelled. "Vitals are stable. She was just pulled out
of the rubble at General American."

Fingers touched her face, probed her eyes. Pain shot
through her as they pried her eyelids apart . . . but she still
only saw darkness.

Sirens approached, and she heard the rumble of an
engine growing near. And then she had the sense of abandonment, as if everyone surrounding her had moved on to
someone else.

"Is anybody there?" She reached around her, groping at
the air. "Please . . . I can't see."

"In a minute, honey," a woman yelled. "We're helping
the more critical patients first."

She thought of Carl, with his crushed legs, maybe even
a broken back, and Andy, with seared lungs.

And others around her, in even worse shape.

Bree knew that time was important if her vision was to be saved, but how could she demand attention when people around her were dying?

She lay there, praying in a loud whisper, begging the Lord to take her blindness away. "If You do, Lord, I promise I'll devote my life to serving You."

But the prayer felt limp and lifeless on her lips, for her faith was weak, and she feared that the Lord had plans to use her blindness.

She thought of Paul on the road to Damascus. He'd been living for himself, and for some made-up God he thought he knew, when the Lord struck him blind. He'd been blind for three days, long enough to realize that the Lord was dealing with him. When his sight was restored, he was never the same again. Was the Lord dealing with her too? Would her sight be restored, or would the time ticking by make it more and more impossible for her to be healed?

Bree stopped the direction of her thoughts and decided to be grateful instead. She had been buried alive, and God had sent someone to rescue her. He knew of her plight.

The truth was that she didn't have an ounce of control over anything that happened. Her eyes, and her family, were in God's hands.

4

CHAOS REIGNED AT THE HOSPITAL AND AMBULANCES bottlenecked in the emergency room drive. Doctors stood in the driveway treating patients as they came out of the ambulances, performing emergency triage, rating the patients according to the severity of their conditions.

Carl moaned as they pulled him out of the rescue unit and surrounded him, evaluating his injuries. "Broken bones in both legs, possible vertebral fractures. Immobilize him and give him something for pain."

"Doctor, can't we get him into X-ray?"

"Yes, but he'll have to wait in line. Life-or-death first."

He started to protest, but the group around him dispersed. Then a nurse ran back with a syringe. She fed it into the IV they had inserted in the ambulance. Would he be paralyzed for the rest of his life? Or would his remaining days be plagued with chronic pain? He thought of

Jacob, who'd wrestled with God and wound up with a dis-
located hip. The Lord had used that in Jacob's life, and had
later made a nation out of that stubborn man. Was this
affliction supposed to bring about some change in Carl's
life? Was he supposed to accept whatever his condition
meant and expect God to work around it?

He didn't want to accept it, any more than he wanted
to work around it. *You saved my life, Lord. Please save
my legs.*

In moments, relief from his pain seeped over him,
and the day grew blurry as he fell into a shallow sleep.

They gave Andy oxygen on the way to the hospital, but
breathing came with great difficulty. Once there, they
did some respiratory tests and inserted a tube from his
nose into his lungs. Then they left him there trying to
breathe.

He lay still, slightly panicked, feeling the assault of
abandonment. If only someone would come back!

Had they been able to help Bree yet? Was Carl in
surgery? Or were they, like him, relegated to the end of
the triage line, waiting their turns for treatment?

At least he had a room, unlike those lying on gurneys

all over the parking lot and in the halls. He'd probably gotten special attention because they considered breathing a life-or-death event and they needed to attach him to this machine.

Still, he felt as lonely as he'd ever felt in his life. Even if he could speak, there was no one to speak to.

He thought of his voice, seared and broken. Would his vocal cords ever be restored, or had he been condemned to silence for the rest of his life? They had worked hard keeping him breathing, but no one had looked at his vocal cords to see what was wrong. What if they waited too long to address that?

He thought of another man who had been struck mute—Zacharias, in the Bible. He'd questioned God one too many times, and in answer had been struck dumb until his son, John the Baptist, was born. Andy had questioned God many times. Was he being punished for that now? Would there be an end to this trial, as there had been for Zacharias? If so, when?

A team of nurses and orderlies rolled another man into the room with him, distracting him from his thoughts. The man was unconscious and lay helpless and silent. Another patient was brought in, this one awake but groaning in pain.

Loneliness gave way to a sense of inadequacy. He longed to help these people whose needs weren't being met, but he couldn't think of a thing he could do for them . . . except pray.

5

BREE HEARD HER NAME CALLED THROUGH THE crowd of injured, and she tried to sit up.

"Bree, thank God you're all right!" Her mother's voice reached her before she did, and Bree groped toward it in her darkness.

"Mommy!"

It was her children's voices. She moaned with shivering relief, and in seconds they were at her gurney, their arms around her.

She clung to them. "You're all right!"

Her mother touched her face with careful hands. "Honey, your eyes . . ."

"I'm blind, Mom. I can't see. And they're so busy with the others . . ."

Her seven-year-old, Amy, began to wail, and Bree

pulled her close again. She wished she could see her face. "What's the matter, honey?"

"I'm scared. Look at your face, Mommy!"

She heard her son sniffing, and she reached out for him too. "You're not crying, are you, Brad? Mommy's okay."

"Your eyes! They need to fix them."

"They will, honey. Real soon."

It sounded as though Bree's mother was crying too. "What can I do for you, sweetie? I want to help you, but I don't know—"

"You can take the children home." Bree kept her voice calm and steady. "Now that we each know the other is all right, you should take them home and let the doctors deal with me here. The kids don't need to see me like this. It's upsetting them."

Her mother pushed her hair back from her face. "But we don't want to leave you."

"It's a madhouse here, Mom. There are too many people. They'll get to me soon. Just go home and pray."

When her mother finally kissed her good-bye and took the children away despite their cries to stay with her, Bree fell back onto her pillow, exhausted but grateful. The Lord had answered two of her prayers: she'd been rescued, and her children were fine. She prayed that someone would come and tend to her wounds soon so that she could go home to her children and hold them as they fell asleep tonight.

Later that night, a doctor made it into her room. He stood beside her bed with his hand on her shoulder, and she wished she could see him. "We're doing surgery on your eyes in the morning," he said, "but there's significant damage."

His weary voice didn't sound hopeful. "Will I see again?" she managed to ask.

There was a long pause. "We'll do the best we can, Ms. Harris."

"What does that mean?"

He sighed. "Nerves have been damaged, and the cornea was lacerated. I'll try to get the glass and metal out and repair as much as I can, but I can't promise that your sight will return."

After he left, Bree lay in the silent darkness that cloaked her. She was too numb to think, too numb even to pray. Finally the pain medication worked through her system, and Bree fell into a dreadful, shallow sleep.

6

THE NEXT MORNING, BREE FELT THE LIGHT OF DAY through the window, warming her face. Slowly, she opened her eyes.

She saw light! She turned her face to the window, where she saw clouds floating through the sky, a tree just beyond the glass. And around her, she saw the other injured patients.

"I can see." She sprang off of her gurney and looked around for a nurse or doctor. "I can *see!*"

Had they done surgery on her last night when she'd been asleep? Wouldn't she have awakened for part of it? Wouldn't she have bandages?

She saw a bathroom, ran into it, and looked into the mirror. The cuts on her face and eyes were gone, and she looked as unharmed as she had yesterday before the quake. How could that be? No surgery could have healed her cuts that quickly, restored her vision, and erased her scars.

She came back out of the bathroom, and a nurse rushed toward her. "You should have called me, honey. I would have helped you."

"I can see! Look at me."

The woman clapped her hands over her own face and stared at Bree. "How can that be?"

"I don't know."

"But they didn't do surgery yet. They didn't do anything!"

Her heart hammered with realization. She had been healed, not by doctors or equipment or cleverly mixed drugs.

God had healed her.

"I'm going to get the doctor!" The nurse raced out the door.

Bree went back to her gurney, looking around for someone else to tell.

On the gurney next to her lay a high-school boy, blood caked on his disfigured face. Clearly frightened and traumatized, he looked up at her and met her eyes.

Flash.

The boy was no longer a teen, but a child, kneeling in a dark attic, screaming and banging at the door to get out.

"Daddy, please let me out. I'll be good. I promise I'll be good."
He had a black eye, and his face was pale as if he hadn't seen
the sun in days.

Flash.

Bree blinked, then stared at the boy, who was once
again a teen, once again stretched out in front of her on
the gurney. What in the world had just happened? Here
she stood, in a busy hospital room, staring at a boy who
had just been through an earthquake, yet she'd seen a little
boy in an attic . . . and she knew it was him.

Had it been a vision of some kind?

She was shaking, she realized, and she turned her eyes
from the boy. "I need to go home."

Her heart pounded as she tried to get away from the
boy whose past she had just glimpsed, and she walked
through the gurneys toward the door.

The nurse bustled back in. "Ma'am, the doctor will be
here soon. You need to lie down until he comes."

Flash.

It was nighttime. She saw the nurse tending to her sick
husband. He was ill and could hardly move for himself.
Vomit stained the sheets, and the woman moved around like
a zombie, exhausted by her work schedule by day and her
caring schedule by night.

"It's okay, honey," she whispered as she stood over her

husband. "*I'll clean it up.*" *She worked the sheet out from under him, cleaned his face and his neck, changed his shirt, then managed to change his sheets out from under him.*

Exhaustion and dejection painted her features as she lay down beside him and slid her arms around him. "*You're going to be okay, honey. I'm here.*"

But he wasn't there, not really, and loneliness radiated from the woman's broken heart.

Flash.

The nurse reached for her to move her back into bed.

Bree started to run, dodging the gurneys, zigzagging through the people, until she finally got out into the sunlight and took off running, running, running, until she came to a convenience store where she went in and asked for a phone.

Desperately glad to be out of that place, she called her mother to come and pick her up.

7

CARL WOKE ON THE SAME GURNEY HE'D BEEN brought in on, still strapped down . . . but the pain was gone. He wiggled his fingers and managed to get one hand free, then felt his legs. They seemed straight and whole.

Wanting to see for himself, he managed to pull the brace off of his neck and slowly sat up and looked down at himself. His pants were still torn, but the blood was gone, and the legs that he'd seen last night—all mangled and bent like pieces of wire twisted in all directions—looked perfectly normal.

Slowly he peeled back the straps holding him to the bed and pulled his legs free. They moved without pain or trouble.

"I can't believe this," he whispered. "How in the world?"

He moved his legs so they hung off of the gurney, then slowly slid his feet down until they bore his weight. He stood on them, expecting searing pain to shoot through them, but there was no pain at all! His legs felt stronger than they'd ever felt before, and an urgent need to move filled him.

"I can walk." He marched across the floor, then jumped and spun around. "I'm healed!"

He knew without a doubt that the Lord had shown him mercy. No doctor had done this. It was clearly an act of God.

He wanted to tell someone, but that urgency to go rose up inside him, drawing him barefoot out of the room. His feet ran and skipped around the gurneys that blocked the hall.

Those feet led him faster, faster than his mind could keep up. They led him between gurneys and around the corner, up the hall. And then they stopped beside the bed of a boy who lay sleeping.

Carl looked down at the child and saw that his lips were blue. His skin looked as gray as death itself.

The boy wasn't breathing.

Carl grabbed his shoulders and shook him. The boy remained limp. "Help!" He yelled at the top of his lungs as he scanned the hallway for a nurse. "This boy isn't breathing. Somebody help!"

A nurse came running, saw the boy's condition, and called out a Code Blue. Doctors and nurses from all over the floor raced toward them to revive the child.

Carl stood back, watching as adrenaline shot through him, twisting around his confusion. How had he known to walk right up to that boy? It was as if his feet had known the child's condition.

How could that be?

He looked down at his bare feet. They looked the same, but something was different. That urge to walk had overcome him again.

He gave into it, and suddenly his feet were making that mad dash again, though he had no idea where they were taking him.

He left the hospital and went out into the bright morning. He started walking in a direction away from his own home, and then picked up his speed until he ran one block, and then another, turned a corner, and went down a hill.

He saw a team of people digging at a collapsed building, still trying to rescue anyone who was buried.

His feet led him to another collapsed building across the street, but no one was digging here. Instead, a crowd of people stood out on the street talking and chattering, as if grateful they had survived the quake.

Carl turned, staring at the rubble. His skin crawled with a certainty so powerful it nearly knocked him down. Someone was in there, trapped in the collapsed building. He grabbed a man on the sidewalk. "Is everyone in this building accounted for?"

The man nodded. "Yes. I work there. I'm pretty sure everyone got out."

Carl knew that wasn't true, though he couldn't have said how he knew. He took off running around to the back of the building where the wall had caved in. The man followed, staring as Carl stepped over the rubble. "How do you get to the basement?"

"Well, there's a stairwell—" he pointed—"but you shouldn't go in there. The building's probably unsound."

Despite the warning, Carl bolted toward the stairwell. He reached it and threw the door open. He started down the stairs . . . then stopped cold.

It was as if the ground had just come up in a heap to swallow up the floor and walls of the basement. There was nothing but dirt and rubble on the side where the building's wall had caved in.

There were people down there. He knew it with absolute certainty.

He ran back up. "Get some workers over here! There are people in there!"

Several of the firemen from across the street came running over and down the stairwell to see the rubble.

"Get some equipment over here!" one of the firemen shouted. "They could be alive."

"They are!" Carl's voice trembled with urgency. "I can tell you right now that they're still alive."

He didn't know how in the world he knew such a thing, but he had no time to question it. He had to get to those people before it was too late. He grabbed a shovel and started digging with the firefighters, determined to rescue these people who had somehow drawn him to their aid.

Within an hour, they made contact with the people who were buried, and one by one they managed to get them out, all alive. One man couldn't feel his legs. Another had a severe head injury and was unconscious. Two came out almost unscathed. When the fourth man came out, Carl knew they were finished. There were no others.

He turned and raced up the street, running like a track star for a couple of blocks, though his lungs panted and gasped for breath. A crowd of people stood in front of a store that sold televisions, and they watched the monitors as the news covered the earthquake damage.

He stopped in that crowd, looking around. He had expected to find another building, more people buried, rescue workers with shovels, but instead there were just people standing and looking at the television monitors, tears on their faces.

He saw a man in the crowd and quickly walked toward him. His feet seemed to know that the man needed help, but Carl stood there not knowing what to say or do. The man gave him an uneasy look.

"May I help you?"

"No . . . uh . . . I'm sorry."

Something strange was happening to him. He felt the man's pain, as if there was something within him that needed rescuing, but Carl didn't have a clue what it was.

He suddenly felt very tired. His head had begun to ache, and he thought about his parents in North Dakota. They had probably been calling his house all night, frantic to know if he was alive.

He needed to get home. He needed to make contact with the important people in his life. He needed to rest.

A tidal wave of weariness and confusion crashed over him, crushing him with its weight until he could barely stand. Trembling, he started walking home.

8

ANDY DIDN'T REALIZE HE'D BEEN HEALED UNTIL his sister and her husband showed up at the hospital that morning. He still had a tube down his throat, but it didn't burn like it had yesterday, and his breathing came easier.

When the doctor made rounds, he pulled the tube out, and it was only then that Andy knew something had happened.

"I couldn't talk at all last night," he said in a rapid-fire cadence. "I'm telling you, I couldn't talk. My throat was burned, and my lungs felt parched, and I had blisters in my mouth and down my trachea. And now there's not a trace of smoke inhalation, not a cough or a wheeze or phlegm in my throat or anything. Do you think I've been healed?"

The doctor looked baffled and went to study his test results again.

Andy looked up at his sister, Karen. "I thought I was a dead man yesterday, and I was in a lot of ways, but I'm telling you something strange happened to me last night. I shouldn't be able to talk at all." He glanced at the man on the bed next to him, who was watching and listening quietly. "Sir, I'm telling you that I was healed miraculously, just like in the Bible. It's almost like Jesus came in and touched me and I was healed, only I don't know why He'd heal *me*, of all people, because I've never been much of a soldier in His kingdom. It's not like I'm worthy of a miraculous healing, but I'm telling you that's what's happened."

Karen started to laugh. "Andy, I don't think I've heard you say that many words in a day, much less in a minute!"

"I know!" Andy swung back around to her. "But all of a sudden I feel like I just have so much to say. I have to tell everybody about the miraculous healing power of a God who cares about us. Jesus is good! I don't know how it happened, but I know *what* happened, and God healed me just as surely as I'm standing here with you."

The doctor came back in, still reading his chart and scratching his head. "I can't explain it. When we looked at your vocal cords and your lungs last night, you were in serious trouble."

"I'm well now!" Andy lifted his hands to the ceiling. "Examine me and you'll see."

The doctor listened to Andy's lungs and looked into his throat. Finally he pulled the stethoscope from his ears and gave Andy a long look. "You can go home, I guess. You look fine to me."

Andy sprang off of the bed, hugged his sister, and slapped his brother-in-law's hand. "I'm outta here."

Karen just stared up at him. "You're not acting like yourself, Andy. Are you sure you didn't hit your head?"

"I was only buried under a three-story building, Karen. I hit my head and everything else. But nothing on me is hurt."

"But you're not acting like yourself."

"I don't know what you mean." He started out into the hall, not even bothering to wait for the paperwork that would release him. When he came through the door, he bumped into a gurney parked there. A woman lay on it, groaning.

He stopped and bent over her. "Ma'am, I'd like to pray for you if you don't mind. See, I was healed, and the Lord who owns the universe and everything in it has the power to heal you too. So I'd like to pray and ask Him to send you the help you need, to comfort and help with your pain."

The woman started to cry. "Get away from me."

A nurse touched his shoulder. "Sir, can I help you?"

"I just wanted to pray for her," he said. "I didn't mean to upset her, but she's obviously in pain, and I thought prayer might be something that would help her because it sure helped me. I didn't mean to offend her."

"She'd rather be left alone," the nurse said calmly. "If you don't mind."

Andy gave a plaintive nod. "Sorry."

He walked to the next gurney and bent over it. "Sir, do you know the Lord? Because I do, and amazingly and miraculously, He healed me this morning after I'd inhaled smoke while buried under a three-story building. And I feel that I have to use my voice now to glorify and praise Him, and what better way to do that than to tell everyone I see about the love of Christ—"

Someone grabbed him and pulled him away from the man. He turned to find it was Karen. She glanced from side to side, as if he'd embarrassed her. "Andy, you've got to stop talking. They're going to call security."

"But there are people who need to hear what happened to me, and I can't stop speaking about what I have seen and heard. I think that's a verse from Acts 4, when Peter and John were arrested and told not to speak anymore about Jesus, and they said they couldn't stop speaking about what they'd seen and heard. I know exactly how they felt now, because as much as I'd like to, I can't seem to stop talking about it."

He pulled away from her then and stopped a nurse coming his way. "Ma'am, do you understand how precious you are in God's sight? Do you know that He knit you in your mother's womb, and that He knew you even before the foundation of the earth was laid?"

"Well . . . uh . . ."

Karen's husband, Ed, grabbed Andy's arm and pulled him away. "Come on, bro. They're going to admit you in the psychiatric ward if you don't shut up right now."

Andy towered over his brother-in-law, but he allowed him to pull him from the building. "You've never told me to shut up in your life, Ed. What's gotten into you?"

"I've never *had* to tell you to shut up! You don't talk much. It's not your nature. You're quiet and pensive and mutter a lot."

Karen grabbed his other arm. "Andy, I know you're excited about being healed, but it wouldn't hurt to rest your vocal cords to keep from straining them again."

"I'm fine." They went down the front steps of the hospital and toward the parking lot. "I'm just realizing that when the Lord gives you a gift, you have to use it for His glory, and I've been given a gift. I've never thought of my voice as being a gift from God, but it is, Karen, and yours and Ed's are too. Only I've had something so amazing happen that I can't help feeling marked by God in some way, like He has a special plan for these vocal cords of mine, and if I'm quiet about it I'll just be throwing that gift back in His face, and besides, I don't think I could hush if I wanted to, because I just have all these words right on the tip of my tongue, and if I don't let them roll off, I think I might wind up in that psych ward, after all."

They got into his sister's car, and he ducked his massive frame into the backseat. "So where were you guys when the quake happened?"

"We were both at home, thankfully," Ed said. "It didn't do too much damage in our part of town."

"Well, what if that had been different?" Andy leaned up on the seat. "What if you had been in a building that collapsed? Say you died. Do you think you would have gone to heaven?"

"I don't know if I believe in an afterlife," Ed muttered.

"What if you're wrong?"

Ed rolled his eyes. "Andy, I can't deal with these hypotheticals right now, okay? I'm just going to take you home."

Andy wasn't daunted. "I'm serious, Ed. You need to think about that, you know. Everybody needs to think about it, especially in light of what just happened. I mean, if you don't believe in an afterlife, you must have reasons for it. But one of us is wrong, and I think it's you."

Ed chuckled. "Well, you're entitled to your beliefs, and I'm entitled to mine."

"We're going to find out someday, Ed. I mean, I survived this, but I'm going to die one day, and so are you."

"Not for a while, I hope."

"Could be today . . . or tomorrow. There could be another quake in the next few minutes, and the ground could swallow us up, and we could all be lying there dead."

Karen's mouth fell open, and she gave him a disgusted look. "Andy!"

"You can't hold off death forever," he went on. "That's my point. There's going to come a time when you're going to find out for sure whether there's a heaven or a hell. Now, while you can, you need to consider Jesus Christ, like it says in Hebrews 3:1. The Bible also says that broad is the way that leads to destruction. That the way to heaven is through a narrow door, and that door is Jesus Christ."

Ed just stared straight ahead as he navigated his way across town. "Whatever you say, Andy."

"I just challenge you to consider it, okay? It's not God's will that any should perish."

Ed pulled the car into Andy's driveway. His small house looked unharmed. He hadn't even considered the possibility that it could have been damaged in the quake.

"Where's your car, Andy?" Karen's effort to change the subject was apparent.

"I guess it was crushed in the quake. I'm not sure. The insurance will probably take care of it soon. Good thing we live in a small town. I can walk just about anywhere I need to go."

"Call us if you need a ride anywhere."

He nodded, but didn't make a move to get out. "Will you both think about what I said? I could get you a Bible if you need it. I have a couple of extra ones."

"No thanks." Ed was more than annoyed.

Andy got out of the car and closed the door, then started to lean in the window to continue the conversation. Ed started pulling out before he could do that.

Andy waved helplessly. "I don't know why you won't listen to me." He knew they couldn't hear, but he felt compelled to say it. "I'm just trying to tell you the greatest news in the world."

Slowly he walked into the house, dropped his keys on

the table, and stared at the phone. He had to call someone. He still had a lot of talking to do. He sat down with
his phone and the telephone book and started through his
list of friends.

He hoped they would listen.

9

THE BROTHERHOOD COMMUNITY CHURCH HAD suffered its own damage in the earthquake. The roof on the northeast corner of the building had caved in. While most of the building still stood, the damage was extensive enough that the leadership feared having the congregation meet in there for the Friday-evening service. Instead, they congregated in the fellowship hall to pray for those still buried in the rubble, for the rescue workers and medical personnel caring for the injured, and for all those grief-stricken people searching for their loved ones tonight.

Bree arrived at the church with her mother and her children and greeted one of the deacons who stood at the door.

Flash.

She saw him as a younger man, walking through a jungle wearing combat fatigues, a gun slung from his shoulder. His

face was painted in camouflage. His comrades walked in
front of and beside him, listening, their guns poised to shoot.

The sound of machine-gun fire startled them all. The
young man next to him hit the ground . . . then another . . .
and another, until he was left standing alone.

A bullet ripped through his leg, and he fell, too, still firing
at some invisible target.

Flash.

"Bree!" The deacon was speaking to her with a huge
smile. "I heard you'd been injured in the crash. I didn't
expect to see you."

Shaken by the vision, she swallowed hard. "Uh . . .
James, are you a veteran, by any chance?"

His face changed, and that smile faded. "Well, yes. I
fought in Vietnam."

Then the visions were true. She felt a little dizzy and
reached out to steady herself.

"Why do you ask?"

"I just . . . heard it somewhere. Come on, kids . . ."

She took her children's hands and escorted them past
him. Tears came into her eyes, but she knew that if she
started crying, she might not be able to stop. Something
was wrong with her. Maybe it was a head injury. Maybe
she did need to be back in the hospital.

Quickly, she took a seat at the back of the room.

Across the room she saw Carl coming in—and she stared. He looked perfectly healthy! The legs that she was sure would be paralyzed strode into the room. Carl didn't even have a scratch on his face. She watched him walk the perimeter of the room, as if he was too fidgety to sit down.

Then she saw Andy filing in with a group of people. He was deep in conversation, and she wasn't able to catch his eye. His voice seemed to be working now.

The service began, and she tried to concentrate on praying. But the moment the service was over, she turned to her mother. "Mom, can you take the kids home? I need to talk to Carl and Andy."

"Sure. Do you want me to put them to bed?"

"No, they can stay up. I'll tuck them in when I get home."

Her mother and children scurried off, and Bree crossed the room to Carl. She hugged him. "Carl, I'm so glad you're okay."

"You too, Bree. Man, I didn't think so when I saw you after they pulled you out. How in the world can you look so good? Your face was cut all over and scraped and bloody, and your eyes were swollen shut."

"And you . . . how are you walking?"

Carl shook his head. "It's the weirdest thing."

"Man, I've got to talk to you two." They both turned and saw Andy towering over them. "Do you have a minute? Something weird has been happening."

Bree frowned. "What do you mean, something weird? Andy, how are you talking?"

"I've been healed—"

"Me too!" Carl said. "Man, I woke up this morning as good as new, like yesterday hadn't even happened."

Bree brought her hand to her face. "And you can see by my eyes that the same thing happened to me!"

"But it's more than that." Andy looked from side to side, keeping his voice low. "Can we go somewhere private and talk?"

Bree hesitated. Something weird, Andy said . . . Had he and Carl been seeing visions too? "Yeah. Let's find a Sunday-school room." She led them out of the fellowship hall and into the hallway.

But Carl wasn't following her lead. He'd turned to go the other way, into a group of people clustered near the exit. She tried to catch up with him, and Andy followed behind her. Carl stopped next to a woman who stood off by herself, listening to the chatter of the group.

When she saw Carl standing beside her, looking as if

he was waiting for something, she got an uncomfortable look on her face. "Can I help you?"

He just stood there. "Uh . . . no."

Then Bree met her eyes.

Flash.

She saw her as a small child, maybe four or five, being dragged, kicking and screaming and crying, from her home and put into a human-services car. Her parents stood at the door cursing and screaming threats at the people who were taking her. She saw the child being belted into the backseat, heard her crying and wailing for her parents as the police snapped handcuffs on them—and dragged them away for drug charges.

Flash.

Bree broke out in a cold sweat as Andy came up behind them.

"Man, there are people out there who need us. We've got to tell them about the Lord," he said. "I mean, we can't expect to just sit in here and have people come to us, you know. I know there were a few new faces in here tonight, but for the most part we've got to go minister to them where they are, because how can they know unless they are told, and how can they be told unless someone is sent, and how can they be sent unless—"

Carl grabbed Andy and headed the other way up the hall. "Come with me."

Andy kept chattering as Carl led them to a room. Bree closed the door and switched on the light.

"Something weird is happening," Andy said again. "I think I'm losing my mind."

"Me too," Carl said. "Don't tell me. You feel like your feet are taking you all over the place, like they know things you don't know, and you can't be still no matter what you do?"

Andy and Bree looked at each other. "That's what's happening to you?" Bree asked.

"Yeah." Carl kept pacing. "Ever since my legs were healed, it's like they have a life of their own. If that's not what you meant, then what's happening to you?"

"I can't shut up," Andy said. "I've been talking people to death. Everybody I see . . . witnessing and quoting Scripture like it's my last day on earth or something. Like I have to cram a lifetime of lost opportunities into one minute."

Bree gaped at them both. "And I see things."

Both men turned to her. "What do you mean?"

"I've been having visions. I mean, really weird visions, like if I look somebody in the eye—not every time, but real often—if I look somebody in the eye I have this flash into his or her life. I see defining moments when something terrible happened. Like that girl outside, Carl, that you were just standing beside. Why did you take us up to her?"

Carl shook his head. "I don't know. It's the weirdest thing. It's like my feet are taking me places I don't want to go, and when I get there I know somebody is in danger, and I feel this urgency. I led some firemen to some people buried under rubble today. How I knew they were there, I don't know. Something supernatural is going on here. I can't stop it, and now I'm walking up to people in crowds and just standing there. I know they need help. I know they're in danger, but I can't seem to figure out what it is I'm supposed to do next. And that girl out there, she was one of them. I just felt like walking up to her, and then I stood there and I didn't know what to do."

"And then I saw a flash into her life," Bree said. "That girl was taken from her parents when she was a tiny little girl. She saw the police arrest her mom and dad on drug charges."

"How do you know that?"

"I told you, it's these visions. I just *saw* it. I've been

seeing into people's lives all day. It's just bizarre, and it's making me crazy."

"I know just what you mean." Andy took her shoulders. "I'm chattering my head off and driving people away left and right, but I can't seem to stop it. And the weird thing is I'm quoting Scripture that I didn't know before."

Bree sat down. "You've only been a Christian for, what, a year?"

"Yeah, and I've always had trouble memorizing. Now all of a sudden I'm quoting Scripture like crazy."

Carl frowned. "You don't think we've been given some kind of supernatural gifts, do you? I mean, God spared our lives, but maybe he also had some wild purpose for our survival."

"It doesn't feel like a special gift." Bree hugged herself. "It feels kind of like a curse. I'm scared of it. I'm almost afraid to look into anybody's eyes."

Andy bent down to her. "Well, why aren't you seeing into my past? You're looking in *my* eyes."

Bree shrugged. "I don't know. It doesn't happen with everybody. I saw a lot of people when I came in here tonight, people greeting me and hugging me and telling me how glad they were that I was all right, and I didn't have the flash then. I only had one flash then—it was of

James Miller in Vietnam. But I sat down after that and didn't look up until the service started."

Carl began to pace again. "So I felt an urgency to walk up to that girl, and then you saw a vision into her past."

Andy stared at the floor, as if piecing the puzzle together there. "Yeah, and then I opened my mouth and started rambling, only I didn't know what she needed to hear."

Carl's eyes widened. "Do you think maybe we're supposed to be working together? I mean, I've been running all over town all day. It's been so weird, and I'm exhausted, and I don't feel very productive, except for that time that I showed the firemen where those people were trapped. Maybe if I had Bree to follow up with her visions into people's lives, and you, Andy, to talk to them, it would make some kind of sense."

"I think you're right." Andy's eyes rounded. "Maybe we're supposed to work together to fill people's spiritual needs and help them see that Christ is the answer. That's the reason we're here, isn't it, to continue the work that Jesus started? Ephesians 2:10 says that we are His workmanship, created in Christ Jesus for good works, which God prepared beforehand, that we should walk in them. And what are those good works supposed to be? Well, of *course* we're supposed to tell people about Christ. I mean, that's our main job as Christians, isn't it?"

Bree stared at the air. "You know, I've only shared Christ with two people in my entire life, and I've been a Christian for fifteen years. Those two people are my children."

"Well, that's nothing to sneeze at," Carl said.

"It's nothing to brag about either. I mean, I've always known I was supposed to bear fruit as a Christian, but I kind of adopted the attitude that people would know by my actions. I just haven't been very proactive. Why in the world would God have chosen me to have a gift like this? Why would He trust me with something like that?"

"I don't know," Carl said. "I don't know why He would choose me, either. I mean, look at me, the short, skinny bald guy, all of a sudden running all over town like an Olympic athlete. You'd think I'd bust an artery or something. I haven't gotten this much exercise in years."

"And me," Andy said. "Quiet Andy. Too cool for conversation most of the time, and here I am, just overflowing with Scripture and wisdom that I don't have."

"Okay, so let's go over this again." Carl walked to the front of the room and used his hands to sort it all out. "I know where to go, and Bree, you know what the problem is because you can see into people's lives. And Andy, once you know the problem, you know what to say."

Andy started to laugh. "Maybe I'm not crazy. Maybe we're all just anointed."

"Anointed?" Bree repeated. "Oh, boy. I'm scared. I'm not a very daring person."

"Well, all you have to do is see," Carl said. "I'll take you to the person; you see the need. Tell Andy what it is, and he'll do the rest. I say we go out right now and test it."

10

"CARL, YOU'RE GOING TO HAVE TO SLOW DOWN!" Bree struggled to keep up with his quick step as he led them blocks away from the church. Andy jogged along beside him, dripping in sweat.

"I'll try," he said. "But I feel like we need to hurry."

"Where are we going, anyway?" Bree looked around them.

"I'm not sure, but my feet know."

Bree laughed. "Do you know how stupid that sounds?"

"Of course I do. It's downright ridiculous, but it happens to be true."

The hospital came into view, and Carl's feet picked up their pace. "Okay, now I've got it. We're going to the hospital."

Bree gasped. "Oh, no! I don't want to go back there."

"Here am I. Send me, Lord," Andy muttered. "We

have to make ourselves available, Bree. That's what we do, we Christians. We're obedient; we go where we're told."

"Theoretically." Bree wished she'd worn more comfortable shoes. Her feet were beginning to hurt.

When they got into the hospital, she looked around and saw that every available space was still occupied by a bed. People lay in various states of consciousness, with head injuries, broken arms, mangled legs. *Everyone* here was in danger. Everyone needed help. How would they ever isolate which person they were supposed to talk to?

But Carl seemed to know where he was going.

He led them through the gurneys to an exit door, then trotted up one flight of stairs, Andy and Bree right on his heels. A doctor walked toward them in the corridor, staring down at a chart.

Carl walked straight up to him, blocking his way.

The doctor looked down at him. "Excuse me." He stepped to his left, but Carl stepped to the right, continuing to block him. Then Bree met the man's eyes.

Flash.

She saw him lying in bed, the alarm clock blaring. His hand trembled as he turned it off, then got out of bed and rubbed his face. She watched as he went to the liquor bottle on his dresser, poured some into a glass, and threw it back.

Flash.

She quickly turned to Andy who stood behind her and whispered one word. "Alcoholic."

Andy stepped up to the doctor, and Carl moved aside. Bree saw that the man's hands trembled, just as they had in her vision.

"You need a drink, don't you?"

Bree blinked at Andy's blunt question, and the doctor gave him a startled look. "What did you say?"

"I said you need a drink, don't you? Bad. But maybe not that bad since you've probably already had a couple of swigs today."

The doctor took a step back. "Look, I don't know who you are, but if you don't get out of my way right now, I'm calling security."

"The Lord sent us here to talk to you, Doctor," Andy said, "and I intend to be obedient. You've sold yourself into slavery to alcohol, but I know how to set you free."

The hardness on the doctor's face melted, and he stepped back against the wall. His mouth began to tremble, and slowly, he seemed to crumble apart.

Then Andy started talking.

Not too long into Andy's conversation, Dr. John Fryer led them into a consultation room. A Gideon Bible sat on a table in the corner, and he grabbed it and began looking up Scripture as Andy quoted it.

Before long, he had given his life to Christ.

As Andy and the others rose to let John Fryer get back to work, he touched Andy's arm. "Do you really think God can deliver me from this alcoholism?"

"I know he can." Andy's voice rang with confidence.

"We have some church members who have beaten addictions," Bree said. "I know if you came there we could hook you up with them and they could help you."

"I've been to AA." John rubbed his eyes. "The twelve steps make a lot of sense, but it's always seemed like there was something missing." He pointed to the Bible. "I think this is it."

"It *is* it," Andy said. "I can promise you that. There's deliverance in the Holy Spirit. Come to church with us Sunday, and we'll introduce you to some people who can help you."

John still had tears on his face as he returned to his work.

Carl grinned and gave Andy a high-five. "That was absolutely awesome, man! I've never seen anything like it. Andy, you did a fabulous job."

"Well, you didn't do so bad yourself." Andy grinned.

"And Bree, the way you saw into that guy's life. I mean you nailed him with one word."

"Yeah, but it wouldn't have done any good if you hadn't been there to follow through. And without Carl, I would have been bouncing all over the place looking into people's eyes and having these weird visions that scared me to death."

"We're a team, man. The dream team," Andy said. "I feel so empowered. That man's life will be changed because of today, and who knows how many other people will be affected by that?"

Carl started leading them back to the stairwell, and they both followed behind him. "Carl, are you doing it again?" Bree asked.

"You got it," Carl said. "Man, I'd love to stop and rest on our laurels, but it looks like there's more work to do."

"Lead us on, man," Andy said.

He led them out of the hospital and to an old apartment complex sporting graffiti on the wall. Vagrants loitered on the sidewalk out front.

Bree hesitated. "I'm kind of scared to come to this place. Are you sure this is where we're supposed to be?"

"Absolutely sure." He started up a flight of stairs, and Bree and Andy tried to keep up.

"Don't be scared, Bree," Andy said. "The Lord says, 'When you pass through the waters, I will be with you; and through the rivers, they will not overflow you. When you walk through the fire, you will not be scorched, nor will the flame burn you.' That's from Isaiah 43:2."

Bree considered the Scripture. "In other words, He's with us, so I don't need to fear."

"That's right."

She nodded. "Okay. Then I won't." She tried to catch her breath. "How many flights, Carl?"

"I don't know. I'll let you know when we get there." He went up two flights, then came around to the walk in front of the doors. He stopped at the third one.

"You're just going to knock on the door?" Bree asked.

"Yeah, and when they answer, you do your bit."

"I have no control over this," she said. "If it happens, it happens."

Carl banged on the door. They heard footsteps across the floor, and then the door cracked open.

"Yes?" A woman with a black eye and busted lip peered through the crack to them. Bree met her eyes.

Flash.

She saw her being beaten up by her husband, kicked and

knocked with his fist until she was down on the floor, scream-
ing for mercy.

Flash.

"Can I help you?" Fear shone in the woman's black
eyes.

Bree stepped forward, trying to be brave. "Uh, ma'am,
I know this sounds really weird, but the Lord sent us here
because your husband beat you up."

The woman opened the door further. "How did you
know that?"

"I told you."

"Don't give me that 'Lord' bit." She peered out past
them. "Did the police send you here?"

"Police?" Bree shook her head. "No. Why would
they?"

"Because they arrested my husband." She started to cry
and stepped back from the door.

Andy stepped inside. "Ma'am, can we come in? We
really need to talk to you."

"Fine, come on in."

They came into her dilapidated apartment and looked
around. The furniture looked like it had come from someone's garage sale, but only after being abused for forty
years. A broken lamp sat in the corner.

The woman sat down, her movements careful, as if less visible parts of her body were broken and injured too. "Now tell me the truth. Why are you here?"

"Ma'am, it's true what we said about the Lord leading us. He cares about you."

She pulled a cigarette from a pack on the table and grabbed a lighter. "If He cares about me so much, then why doesn't He just let me die?"

"He must not be ready for you to die," Andy said. "We're here to tell you how you can live."

"How I can live?" She took a drag of the cigarette and blew it out slowly. "A better question is *where* I can live since my husband got hauled off to jail for beating the stew out of me. I don't have the money to pay my rent that's due on the first of the month. That gives me about five days to find another place to live." She tapped the ashes of her cigarette into an empty beer can. "Oh, and did I mention that I don't have a job?"

"What's your name, ma'am?"

"Sarah Manning."

Andy made formal introductions of the three of them, then quoted the Scripture about how God provides for the birds of the air and the flowers of the field, and then he told her about the ultimate provision God had made for her.

After a while the woman's angry, defeated tears turned to tears of wonder. Her heart seemed to soften, and she began to hang on Andy's every word.

Finally, she agreed to meet them at church on Sunday.

As they started to leave, she came to the door with them. "I think you were right. God really did send you here to me tonight. I wish you had come in time to save my husband too."

"It's not too late for your husband," Andy said. "We have people at our church who do prison ministry. Maybe we can send someone to help him."

The woman dabbed at her eyes. "Looks like God is into miracles these days. Who knows? Maybe He has one for him."

As they left the old apartment complex, Andy and Carl slapped hands again.

"That was just as cool as the first one," Carl said. His step was slower than it had been earlier. "But you know we have to help her. Besides her spiritual needs, she needs a place to live, a job, and money."

"Yeah." Bree looked back at the woman's door. "Makes you wonder, doesn't it?"

"Wonder what?" Andy asked.

"Well, if God gave us these gifts, it makes you wonder

if He didn't give others gifts that would follow these up? Maybe we just haven't found them yet."

"Could be," Andy said. "We'll just have to keep our eyes open."

Carl came to a corner and stopped walking. "Man, I'm exhausted. I feel like I've spent the whole day running a marathon. I could just fall on the sidewalk right here and go to sleep."

"I need to get home, anyway." Bree looked at her watch. "I promised to put my kids to bed. I think I just need to lie down with them and cuddle up for a while. Maybe we could start again tomorrow."

"Sounds good to me."

They headed back to the church. A comfortable silence fell over them as they strolled back with no particular urgency. When they got there, they stood looking at each other for a moment.

"What do you think?" Bree looked from Andy to Carl. "Tomorrow's Saturday. Do we get back together and try it again?"

"Sounds good to me." Carl slumped against his rental car. "My feet are going to be taking me places whether you guys are along or not. You might as well come so we can get something done."

Before they separated they prayed for Dr. John Fryer and Sarah Manning, who'd just accepted Christ. They prayed that the Holy Spirit would do His work to comfort them tonight and keep them firmly planted in their new-found salvation.

11

THE NEXT DAY, BREE'S MOTHER OFFERED TO KEEP her kids while she went out "witnessing" with Andy and Carl. It had occurred to Bree that perhaps she should tell her mother about the extraordinary gift she'd been given, but her mother tended to be an alarmist, and Bree didn't want her thinking that her daughter had some kind of brain injury and rush her to the emergency room. She also didn't want her children to absorb any anxiety from their grandmother. So she chose to keep the matter to herself.

She met Andy and Carl in the church parking lot. Carl paced back and forth, raring to go, and Andy chattered nonstop. When Bree got out of her mother's car, Carl yelled out, "Okay, you're here. Let's go. Hurry!"

"Hurry?" Bree locked her purse in the trunk of her car. "Hurry where?"

"I don't know! I'm just ready to go."

She dropped her keys into her pocket. "Okay. Feet . . . take us away."

Carl shot her an unappreciative look and started walking.

"Don't mock him," Andy said. "'He who mocks the poor reproaches his Maker.' Proverbs 17:5."

"Hey, I'm not poor," Carl said, breathing faster as his step picked up. "I probably make the same thing you make."

"Well, I'm poor," Andy said.

"Me too," Bree piped in. "Dirt poor. I'm the one who has to live with her mother."

"'Blessed are the poor in spirit,'" Andy said. "Matthew 5:3."

"We're not talking about poor in spirit." Bree was glad she'd worn her walking shoes today. "I'm talking poor in wallet. And now I've got to get a new car, and the insurance almost never gives you what your car is worth."

"What did we tell Sarah Manning last night?" Andy breathed hard as he kept up with Carl. "That God provides. 'But seek first His kingdom and His righteousness; and all these things shall be added to you.' Matthew 6:33."

Carl turned and took off up a hill.

Bree trotted behind him. "I'm glad this is a small town. Can't your feet press an accelerator instead of pavement, Carl? We could use my mother's car."

"I think I have to walk. But don't worry. We're here." He led them into another older, deteriorating neighborhood and turned up a sidewalk. "Someone inside this house needs us."

Bree thought of Sarah Manning last night, thanking them for coming. She drew in a deep breath for courage. "Okay. Go."

Carl knocked and stepped back, letting Bree have center stage.

But no one answered. Bree tried again.

Finally, they heard a voice from deep in the house. "Help! Somebody, please help!"

Bree shot an alarmed look to Andy and quickly turned the doorknob. It was unlocked, so she pushed the door open. "Hello?"

"In here."

A woman's weak voice came from the kitchen. Carl bolted through the house and led them to an old woman lying on the floor.

"Thank God you've come . . ." Her words were slurred.

Flash.

Bree saw the woman lying on the floor, trying to get up, but one side was paralyzed. She'd had a stroke, and no one was there to help her. Bree watched her turn to her paralyzed side and push up with her good hand until she managed to get to her feet. She took a step and fell again.

"God! Can You see me at all? Are You there? Do You remember me?"

Flash.

"Call an ambulance," Bree said. "She's had a stroke. Ma'am, how long have you been lying here?"

"Since yesterday." The left side of her mouth didn't move with her right as she spoke.

Bree and Andy got the trembling woman up and carried her to the couch while Carl called for the ambulance.

"God sent you." She turned her faded eyes to Bree's face. "I prayed and prayed for help." She reached out a trembling hand. "I'm May Sullivan."

They each introduced themselves.

"Yesterday, when she couldn't get up, she felt like the Lord forgot her," Bree whispered to Andy, who took the baton.

"Ma'am, do you know the Lord?"

"He knows me." May chewed out the words. "Sure seems to, don't He?"

"Yes, ma'am, He does." Andy's words were soft and gentle. "But He doesn't just want you to get medical help. He wants your spirit healed too. Ma'am, the Lord wants me to tell you what it says in Isaiah 49, verses 14 through 16: 'But Zion said, "The LORD has forsaken me, and the Lord has forgotten me." Can a woman forget her nursing child, and have no compassion on the son of her womb? Even these may forget, but I will not forget you. Behold, I have inscribed you on the palms of My hands.'"

Tears began to run down the woman's half-paralyzed face, and Bree heard a siren approaching the street. The woman reached out for Andy's hand. "Come to the hospital with me. I need to hear more of what the Lord is saying to me. I did think He'd forgotten me. But He ain't, has He?"

"No, ma'am. He hasn't forgotten. We'll come with you and finish this conversation."

The paramedics were the same ones who had rushed Bree to the hospital the day before, and because she pleaded with them—and they were so amazed that she had walked out of the hospital without any of the injuries with which they'd taken her in—they broke the rules and allowed all three of them to ride with the woman to the hospital.

Bree and her friends waited with May, and Andy told her of God's love and the fact that He'd never had her out of His sight. When she had been admitted, they promised to come back and visit her later. She hugged them good-bye as if they were family.

As they left the hospital, they ran into Dr. John again. "Hey, guys." He looked better than he had yesterday, and Bree was certain he was sober, though his hands trembled slightly, and his skin had a gray cast. She supposed his body would have to adjust to its new state. "Were you looking for me?"

"No," Bree said. "We just brought a friend in. She had a stroke, and we found her on the floor of her kitchen."

"What's her name?" Dr. John asked.

"May Sullivan. She's in room 413."

"I'll stop by and see her. So . . . about church tomorrow. I was going to call you."

"You're not backing out are you?" Andy asked. "Come on, man, you need to be there."

"I know." He raised his hands in a mock vow. "I'm going. I just wanted to make sure you didn't forget. I hate going in places like that by myself. I haven't been to church since my best friend's wedding. That was six years ago."

"We'll meet you on the front steps," Carl said. "You won't be the only one. There are a few others we'll be meeting too."

"Great." He patted Carl's shoulder. "I'll be there."

Carl was already starting to walk off, and Bree knew he'd been hit again with that foot thing. So she said good-bye to Dr. John and took off following him. Andy was close behind.

They hurried out of the hospital and up the sidewalk, and Bree shook her head. Where in the world would Carl's feet lead them now?

12

CARL DIDN'T LEAVE THE HOSPITAL CAMPUS. INSTEAD he led them around the building to the courtyard beside a pond, where patients and staff members sat on benches, smoking their cigarettes or staring at the water. Carl's step slowed as he reached a man who sat facing the water, his arms crossed, a stricken, pained look on his face.

"Him?" Bree asked, and Carl nodded.

Bree stepped up to the man. "Excuse me, sir?"

He looked up, and met her eyes.

Flash.

She saw him holding his wife in a dark hospital room, lit only by the night light above her bed. She wept against his chest, and he wept with her. "My baby. Everything was going to be so perfect. One more week, and he would have been born. One lousy earthquake changed everything."

"At least you're all right." The man's voice was pained, strained.

"I wish I was dead," she said. "I want my baby."

Flash.

"Do I know you?" The man frowned up at them.

"Uh . . . no." Bree wondered how to proceed. She couldn't very well tell Andy what was wrong right in front of the man. No, she was going to have to start this herself. "I'm so sorry about the death of your baby. How did it happen?"

He shook his head. "The earthquake. My wife fell when our floor caved in. It's a wonder she wasn't killed too."

Bree looked up at Andy.

He took the seat on the other side of the man, then held out his hand. "Hi, sir. My name's Andy Hendrix. Do you mind if I sit down for a minute?"

The man shook Andy's hand. "Sam Jones. No, I guess not."

"I don't know if you've ever read Psalm 116:15, but it says that 'precious in the sight of the LORD is the death of His godly ones.'"

Sam brought his wet eyes to Andy. "It's not so precious to me."

"No, it never is to us, but your baby's in heaven, and you have the opportunity to see her again."

"Him." Sam cleared his throat. "He was my son." He started to weep again and covered his face to hide it from them.

Andy touched his back. "God understands your pain. His Son died too. An excruciating, cruel kind of death."

The man looked up at him, his features twisted. "I know all about the cross. Never made any sense to me. And the bit about God giving up His only son . . . If there *were* a God, why would He do that? Why would He let Him die?"

"He let Him die because that was why He was born," Andy said. "Jesus came for one purpose: to die so we wouldn't have to."

"Then why do we?" Sam challenged. "If He came to die for us, then why isn't my son alive? Why aren't my parents still here? Why do I have to visit them at their graves?"

Bree watched Andy, waiting to see his answer. She wasn't sure she could have answered that herself.

"It all goes back to Genesis," Andy said. "When man fell. He had a perfect world, and then Satan tempted him. Told him he could be like God and that he wouldn't die. But Adam died, and so did Eve, and so has everyone in the world since that time. Jesus came to stop that cycle, to give us a chance to live, to take on Himself the punishment that we've all deserved because we've all sinned. Hebrews 5:8–9 says that, 'Although He was a Son, He learned obedience from the things which He suffered. And having been made perfect, He became to all those who obey Him the source of eternal salvation.'"

"Obey Him in what? What has God ever asked me to do for Him?"

"Obey by believing in Him. If you do that, we're told that we do not grieve as those who have no hope. That when Jesus comes again, the dead shall rise first. Yes, your little son will rise first, and then you'll join him in the clouds. We'll be caught up together with him in the clouds to meet the Lord in the air, and we'll always be with the Lord."

"Jesus is coming again?" Sam shook his head. "I don't even know if I believe He came the first time."

"I'm betting my eternity on it," Andy said. "So are you, whether you do it consciously or not."

The man stood. "I have to go back to my wife. She needs me. I just came out to get some air." He looked at Andy, then Carl and Bree. "I appreciate you talking to me like this, but I'm not much into religion, you know?"

Andy sprang up. "We go to Brotherhood Community Church. Our service is at 11:00 tomorrow morning. If you can, try to come. At least hear the Lord out. He's after you. He sent us to talk to you because He knows the pain you're suffering."

Sam nodded and offered them a weak wave. "Thanks. I'll think about it. My wife's getting out this afternoon, though. I don't think I can leave her that soon."

They watched him as he headed back up to the hospital, his head hung low.

"So much pain," Bree whispered. "I wish you could have helped him. But I guess even a supernatural gift can't do miracles."

"Of course it can," Andy said. "We planted some seeds. I'm sure of it. The Lord led us here as a team, just like He's done with all the others. It wasn't in vain."

"So should we check on him later, or what?"

"Let's just see what God urges us to do." Andy grinned. "He'll let Carl's feet know."

Already, Carl had started walking, and Bree and Andy followed.

13

THEY SAW SIX MORE PEOPLE ACCEPT CHRIST BEFORE the day was over, and planted seeds in the hearts of eight others. The next morning, Bree, Andy, and Carl showed up early for church, hoping to talk to their pastor before Sunday school and church began.

They found him in his office, going over his sermon notes. Carl knocked on the door, and the pastor looked up.

"Hey, Jim," Carl said. "Can we talk to you for a minute?"

Jim got to his feet and laughed as he saw the three of them. "Well, sure. Come on in. I always have time for the miracle trio."

"The miracle trio?" Bree shot Carl and Andy a look. "Why do you call us that?"

"Because that's what you are. Pulled out of the rubble after being buried for five hours? And not one of you hurt? It's a miracle, that's all there is to it."

"Oh, yeah," Bree said. "I guess you're right. I thought you meant . . . something else."

"Something else?" He laughed. "Like what?"

Bree sat down, and Carl and Andy took seats on either side of her.

"Well, see, uh . . . it's like this," Carl began.

Andy blurted it out. "We've been given some real strange supernatural gifts, and we've been sharing Christ and seeing lost souls turn to Him all over town."

Jim frowned. "Supernatural gifts? What do you mean?"

Andy looked at the others. "I mean . . . we can do things that we couldn't do before. Soul-winning things. Fruit-bearing things."

"Well, that's great." Jim clapped his hands. "That means you're growing. I could tell last week when you said you were starting a Bible study at your office that you were growing and stretching. I've been so proud of you guys."

"No, that's not the kind of gift he means." Bree shifted in her seat. "Not the plain old ordinary work-of-the-Holy-Spirit kind of gift."

Jim laughed out loud. "The 'plain old ordinary work of the Holy Spirit'? Bree, you've got to be kidding. There's nothing about the work of the Holy Spirit that's ordinary."

"I just mean—"

"She means that we're doing some really bizarre things," Carl said. "I have this walking thing. My feet just start walking, and I find these people who need our help."

"Well, that's good, Carl. That's great. We should all be willing to go where the Lord wants to send us."

Bree wanted to shake him. "But I have this vision thing. I can look in someone's eyes, and I see pain and loneliness and things in their lives that have made them into who they are."

Clearly, Jim loved it. "The Holy Spirit is making you sensitive to other people, Bree. See? There's nothing ordinary about that. Yes, it's supernatural. It sure is."

He wasn't getting it. Bree looked at the others. "But Andy is talking, saying things he never would have said."

"Yeah, man," Andy piped in. "I'm quoting Scripture like crazy and teaching and explaining the gospel like I never could before."

"Because you've been studying your Bible," Jim said. "See, Andy? I told you that the more you knew, the more confidence you would have to talk to others. You've always had a teaching gift. That's why I encouraged you to lead the Bible study at your office."

A knock sounded on the door, and Stanley, the choir director, leaned in the door. "Jim, can I see you for a minute?"

He got up. "Excuse me, guys, I'll be right back."

When he was gone, they sat staring at each other.

"Do you believe that?" Bree asked.

Andy started to laugh. Bree joined in, and Carl followed.

"He doesn't get it. He thinks we're just doing regular Christian things."

"I don't know why," Carl said. "We never did them before."

"Well, maybe this is another God thing," Andy said. "Maybe we're not supposed to tell anyone. Maybe we're just supposed to be obedient and keep it all to ourselves."

Bree got up, went to the doorway, and looked out into the hall. "Do you think so?"

"I don't know," Carl said. "Hardly matters, though, if he isn't hearing what we're saying."

Jim came back in and slipped back into his chair. "Sorry. Sound problems. We're expecting a big crowd today, after the earthquake and all. Now, where were we?"

Andy looked at the others, then drew in a deep breath. "We just wanted to let you know that a bunch of the people who have come to Christ in the past couple of days will be visiting our church this morning."

Jim clapped his hands together again. "Great. What are their names? I'll make sure I meet them."

Bree smiled. "Well, uh . . . there are about a dozen of them, I think."

"No, fifteen, I'm pretty sure," Carl said. "They may not all come."

"Fifteen, if you just count the ones who gave their lives to Christ," Andy said. "But some of the seeds God planted could take a little root. A few of those could come too. Could even be twenty or so."

Jim straightened slowly in his chair. "You guys have talked to twenty people about Christ? What . . . did you speak to a rally this weekend or something?"

"No," Bree said. "We've just used our gifts. The ones we told you about."

Jim stood up. "This is amazing. This is just what I needed to hear. My message today is designed for the seeker and the new believer. I wanted to take the opportunity the earthquake gave us to reach those whose hearts were made tender by the disaster."

Carl began to laugh. "Well, we're bringing them so you can preach to them. Only some of them have some pretty serious problems. There's a doctor who's an alcoholic and a woman whose husband abused her."

"The husband's in jail," Bree added. "And she wants us to talk to him . . . only I don't think they'll let us visit him until he's been there a while."

"There's a man whose wife lost her baby in the quake," Andy said. "And then there's May—"

"May?"

"Yes. May's an old woman we found who'd had a stroke and lay on the floor over twenty-four hours. She's in the hospital. She might watch us from television."

"Okay." Jim paced back and forth. "I think I'm getting the picture now."

Bree sighed in relief. "You are?"

"Yes. We can't just stop with a sermon. We have to set up a kind of spiritual triage. These people are hurting. We have to rely on all of the parts of the Body. We have people who can help with grief, and others who've kicked alcoholism, and we have a group who does prison ministry, and there are dozens in the church who are great at serving . . . taking food and giving rides and checking on the elderly."

Bree looked at Carl. "People with gifts that follow up where ours leave off."

"That's right," Jim said. "We're all gifted differently, for just this kind of thing. Trust the Body, Bree. Let it work. I'm so glad you gave me a heads-up this morning. I'll use the Sunday-school hour to go around and gather up some help. Keep bringing them in, guys, and we'll take care of them here. They won't leave this place without knowing how much the Lord loves them."

"Thanks, Jim. We knew we could count on you."

"No. Thank *you.*" He came around the desk and hugged each of them. "One of the things you learn in seminary is that the true test of the effectiveness of your ministry is when you see your fruit bearing fruit. You're doing it, guys. You don't know how much that means to me."

14

B Y THE TIME BREE, CARL, AND ANDY MADE IT TO the front steps where their visitors were to meet them, Sarah Manning was already there. Her eye was still swollen and black, but it was clear that she'd tried her best to hide her injuries with the deft stroke of a make-up brush. She looked awkward and out of place.

Bree hurried toward her. "Hi, Sarah. I'm sorry I wasn't out here sooner. I was talking to the pastor. I hope you had the chance to meet some of our members."

"I sure did." Sarah looked around. "That's the problem. I'm not used to all this. I'm kind of the type that likes to keep to myself, you know? I don't like crowds or a lot of people." She seemed jittery, like she needed a cigarette. "I don't know if this church thing is going to work out for me. I mean, I still want to be a Christian and all, but I just don't know if I can do this crowd stuff every week."

Bree looked around, wondering which of the members had insulted her. "Was someone rude to you?"

"Oh, no, they weren't rude. I got, like, three invitations to lunch, and several invited me to sit with them. And I don't know. I just kind of freaked out. I didn't think I could handle it anymore. I was just about to leave."

Relief and gratitude flooded over her. So none of them had undone her efforts with Sarah. She was just overcome by the love.

"They're just trying to love you," Bree said. "It's what they do at church, at least when church is working well. Don't hold it against them."

"Oh, I don't." Sarah hugged herself. "It just blew my mind. I've never seen anything like that. It's just going to take some getting used to."

"I'll stay with you, but please say you won't leave. God brought you here for a reason. Some day you'll think of these people as family."

Sarah's smile was tentative. "All right, I'll stay."

Bree wanted to hug her, but she feared making her change her mind. Behind Sarah, she saw Carl and Andy with the others who had come, and she recognized the man whose baby had died. A lump of emotion formed in her throat. She hadn't expected to see him again.

"Come over here." She took Sarah's hand and led her toward them. "I have some people I want you to meet."

She could almost feel the woman stiffening beside her as they headed to the group. But as she made the introductions, she felt Sarah relaxing. It was clear that the others were as nervous and uncomfortable as she.

Jim preached the best sermon of his life that morning. Bree sat among the people they'd met in the last couple of days. Sarah sat next to her, riveted on every word the pastor said. Her awkwardness seemed to have melted, and when the altar call came, she got up and went to the front. Bree sat stunned in her seat, amazed by the Holy Spirit's work to make her take such a public stand. Several of the others went, as well.

When the service was over, Bree wiped her tears, then hurried to find Sarah in the back.

Sarah was dabbing at her own eyes, but she had a serene smile on her face.

Bree had to laugh. "That took a lot of courage."

Sarah shook her head. "I think it would have taken more courage to sit there and not go."

"You seem more relaxed now."

"Yeah. Church was different than I thought. I expected people to be judging me, but they weren't, you know? They were nice."

"Listen, why don't you come home with my family and me and eat lunch? I mean, it won't be much. Tuna sandwiches, probably, but the kids and my mother and I would love to have you."

Sarah glanced at the exit door, then brought her big eyes back to Bree. "I don't know. I'm not too good with kids."

As if on cue, Bree's children came running up to her. "Mom, Mom! Can we go home with Danny and his family?"

"Both of you?" she asked.

Danny's age fell between the two of them, so they'd all been close friends since they were in the nursery together.

"Did Danny ask you, or did his parents ask?"

"His parents," her son said. "Mom, please? We never get to do this."

Bree had hoped to go to the hospital to look in on May today. "Well, let me talk to Danny's parents."

Her children ran and got Jeanine, the boy's mother. "Let them come home with us, Bree," Jeanine said. "Heaven knows, you need a break with all that you've been through lately."

"Well, I just feel like I haven't been spending enough time with them."

"Mom, we can have quality time later!" Amy cried. "Come on. Let us go."

Jeanine laughed. "We can keep them all afternoon, then bring them back to church tonight. You can take them home then. It'll be fun. They'll have a good time."

Bree grinned down at her children. "Okay, but give me a kiss." She hugged and kissed both of them, then watched them scurry off.

When they were gone, she turned back to Sarah. "Well, now that I don't need to go home, I think I might just give my mother some quiet time to herself and walk to the hospital to visit a friend. Do you want to come? We could get a bite to eat there. My treat."

Sarah thought that over. "I guess that would be all right."

"Are you sure the crowd at the hospital won't bother you?"

"Oh, yeah, it's not that. It's these people . . . loving me, you know. I'm not used to that."

They started to walk out of the church and headed toward the hospital. Bree studied Sarah. "So you don't mind strangers. You just don't know how to react to people who want to be close to you?"

"Yeah," Sarah said. "I know it's stupid. I probably need

therapy. I *know* I need therapy. It's been a long time since I've had anybody really show me any affection, and today I must have gotten like eighty-nine hugs. Usually when someone comes at me, it's with a fist."

It was a beautiful day, and a breeze whispered through their hair. The sun shone with such serenity that no one would ever know there were things in the world like earthquakes and fires, and people who beat up defenseless women.

"Why would you marry a guy like that?" Bree asked. "I'm just curious. You're a real pretty lady, and you have a sweet spirit. I don't understand why you would bond yourself with somebody like that."

"That's the million-dollar question, and I'd love to have it answered. But here I am, and the truth is, every major relationship I've had has been like this. Men always woo me in the beginning. I start thinking he's just what I've been looking for, the fulfillment of all my dreams, and then I wind up sleeping with him. The next thing I know, my face becomes his favorite punching bag."

"Did you know your husband was abusive before you married him?"

"Yeah, I pretty much did. Kind of felt like I deserved it, you know? Like I did stupid things that caused him to hit me. I thought I could change him. But it never happens that way."

They reached the doors of the hospital and went in, quickly ate a bite, then headed up to May's hospital room.

"You don't have to come in with me," Bree said. "You can wait out here."

"That's okay." Sarah kept walking with her. "I'll come. You said this is a lonely old woman. Wouldn't hurt for me to make friends with somebody as lonely as me. Just as long as you're sure she won't reach out to hug me."

Bree started to laugh. "I'm sure. She's pretty helpless right now."

They got to her room, and May sat up in bed, carefully trying to feed herself with her left hand. But the food kept dribbling out on the stroke side of her mouth.

"How are you today, May?" Bree asked as she came in.

May looked up. "Oh, my rescuer! Come in here, darling. Come in."

Bree came to her side and leaned over to give her a hug. "How are you feeling today?"

"So much better." She looked at Sarah over Bree's shoulder. "And who is this?"

"This is Sarah Manning. She's a new friend, like you."

"Ain't she wonderful?" May asked Sarah, nodding

toward Bree. "You know, she saved my life, she and her two friends. They just showed up at my door when I'd been laying on the floor praying my guts out that somebody would come."

"I heard," Sarah said, "but you look wonderful today."

"I *feel* wonderful. Oh, that Dr. John, he said he knew you and that was why he came by. He's took over my case. He got me the help I need, and he's just a wonderful man."

"Really? John Fryer?"

"Yes. Oh, he's such a giving person . . . so attentive. I've never had a doctor that attentive."

"Wow."

May brought her hand to her heart. "And we talked about the Lord."

"You did?"

"Of course we did. He said that you had helped him turn to Christ, and that his whole life had changed. He told me about the drinking. He's gonna give it up. I know he's gonna kick it."

"Of course he is," Bree said. "But I'm kind of surprised. It just happened yesterday, and already he's reaching out and giving of himself? That's pretty amazing."

"It's a miracle, that's what it is!" May slapped her hand

on the bed. "Another one of God's miracles, just like sending you to me. We've struck up a friendship, Dr. John and me, and I think it's going to last a long time."

She reached out for Sarah's hand and pulled her closer. "Now, tell me about you, dear."

"Well, I guess I'm another one of Bree's converts," Sarah said in a soft voice. "I was like you. I was kind of in my house praying to God for help. My husband had beaten me up, and he was arrested that night, and I realized I was probably not going to have the money to pay my rent, and I wasn't going to have a place to live, and all of a sudden, what do you know? These three people knock on my door and come in and tell me that somebody loves me." Her voice broke, and tears came to her eyes. "I'm sorry," she said, quickly rallying. "I didn't mean to do that."

"Mean to do what?" May asked. "Cry? Well, honey, everybody needs to cry now and then."

"I know, but not in front of strangers."

"Well, I'm not a stranger," May said. "I'm your sister in Christ. Don't you know that?"

Sarah smiled and dabbed at her eyes.

"Now what's this about you not having a place to live?"

Bree jumped in. "Her husband was arrested after he beat her up. She can't afford to pay the rent."

Sarah nodded. "It's due tomorrow, and I don't have the money. It's a dump, anyway. Landlord has already found new tenants, so I have to move out. I'm sure I'll find some place to go. I'll probably go to a women's shelter until I can find a job."

May's face lit up. "Well, why don't you stay in my house?"

Bree caught her breath. "May, are you sure?"

"Of course I'm sure. There's my house, sitting there all empty. As long as I'm in the hospital, I need somebody to look after it." She turned back to Sarah. "You might as well sleep there. I have a guest room, so you can even stay when I get home, and maybe you can give me a hand now and then."

Sarah slowly sat down on the chair next to the bed. "Do you mean that?"

"Of course I mean it. You'd be helping me. I can't go home alone. I'll have to learn to walk again, and it's not gonna be easy. Sarah, do you drive?"

"Yes ma'am," Sarah said, "but I don't have a car. It got repossessed a couple of weeks ago."

"Well, maybe you could drive mine and get me to

physical therapy every day. I mean, until you get a job."
May caught her breath as another thought occurred to her.
"On second thought, *I* could give you a job. You can be
my personal helper until I can get on my feet! What do
you think of that?"

Sarah's eyes filled with tears as she looked from May to
Bree, and back again. "I think that's the most amazing thing
I've ever heard in my life. Talk about answered prayers."

"Prayer works," Bree whispered. She had tears in her
own eyes as she leaned over and hugged May. "You don't
know what this has meant to me."

"To you?" May asked. "I wouldn't even be here if it
weren't for you. It means life to me."

"Abundant life." Bree's throat constricted, and she
swallowed hard. "We told you, didn't we?"

Sarah laughed softly. "Man, you sure did."

They heard footsteps running up the hall, then Carl
squeaked around the doorway, his tennis shoes almost
skidding across the floor.

"Bree, I thought I'd find you here." He was so out of
breath he could hardly speak. "I have to go. I have to go
now."

Bree turned back to Sarah and May. "I need to go with
him. I think there's somebody else who needs us."

"Sure. Go," May said. "You do what you gotta do."

"Yeah," Sarah said. "I'll just stay here and get to know May a little bit better."

Bree grinned as she followed Carl out the door. Andy was just coming off of the stairwell when they walked out into the hall.

"Man, you're getting faster," he said to Carl. Carl was already heading back down the stairs.

"You guys won't believe what just happened," Bree said as she ran down the stairs. "I brought Sarah here to have lunch, and then we went up to see May, and the next thing I know, May's telling me how Dr. John Fryer has been ministering to her and taking care of her."

"Really?" Andy mopped the sweat off of his face with his sleeve.

"Yeah, but get this: Sarah's sitting there telling May that she doesn't have a place to live, and the next thing you know, May is inviting her to come live with her! Then Sarah mentions that she doesn't have a job, and May hires her to be her assistant when she gets home."

Carl looked back over his shoulder. "No way. Are you kidding me?"

"I'm not kidding. This is all working out, just like Jim said. Our fruit is bearing fruit. Can you imagine?"

"Did you see what happened at church today?" Carl turned a corner. "I've never seen anything like that in my life. Every one of the people we brought got ministered to. Some of them even went home with church members. I noticed that Dr. John went home with Greg Browning."

Bree gasped. She knew that Greg Browning had almost drunk himself to death years ago, but he hadn't had a drink in over seven years. "That's great! He's just the one I wanted to introduce Dr. John to."

Carl nodded. "If anybody can help John, it's him."

"That's nothing," Andy said. "I saw Sam Jones—the man whose wife lost their baby—going home with Dennis Simmons and his wife. They lost their baby last year."

"Oh, that's perfect!" Bree punched at the air. "The Simmonses will be able to help so much with that family."

"I think so." Carl breathed as hard as Bree and Andy, but his feet seemed to move faster and faster.

"Carl, can you slow down just a little?"

"I don't think so," Carl said, so Bree broke into a trot. She should have changed her shoes after church, she thought. Carl finally took them into a pretty, middle-class neighborhood with well-groomed lawns and houses that were only a year or two old. Bree frowned. From her lower middle-class home with her mother, she had often wondered if people who lived in houses like these really ever had any problems. And yet, here they were, beating the pavement, a holy task force headed to rescue another soul. They rounded a corner, and a house came into view with cars parked along the street and filling the driveway. People came and went with covered dishes in their hands.

"Looks like somebody is having a party," Andy said.

Carl turned up the sidewalk. "That's where we're going. Right there. That's the house."

"No." Bree grabbed him by the shirt and tried to stop him. "Carl, we can't go in there. Look at them. They're having a party. How would we know which person needs us?"

"I don't know, but this is where God is telling me to go. And trust me. It's very urgent."

Bree groaned and looked at Andy.

"We might as well follow him," Andy said. "He hasn't led us wrong yet."

So they trudged up the sidewalk toward the front door. And just as they reached the front steps, a woman came out. She was wearing a black dress and had tears on her face.

Bree stopped. "Hello."

The woman covered her mouth. "It's terrible, isn't it? A real tragedy." Then she headed out to her car.

Looking back at the woman, Carl stopped at the front door, his chest heaving. "Did you see anything when you looked at her, Bree?"

"No," Bree said, "but I'm getting a feeling that maybe this isn't a party, after all."

"Funeral." Andy watched the woman's car drive away. "It's a funeral."

"How do you know?"

"Well, look what everybody's wearing." He nodded to a group who had come out the side door. "Mostly black."

Bree saw it now. "Oh, they sure are. You think it's for someone who died in the earthquake?"

"Maybe," Carl said. "It could be ours, if God hadn't rescued us."

Bree's throat constricted. She thought of her mother grieving, her children clutched together, mourning over their lost mother.

Why had she been spared, and someone in this house had not? She forced herself to step up to the door, but Carl stopped her.

"Wait. I thought this was it, but it isn't."

"Oh, thank goodness. I didn't know what to say—"

"I mean, it's the house all right, but not inside." He led them down the porch steps and started around the back of the brick house.

"Carl, where are you going? You can't just walk into people's backyards. We're trespassing." But Carl wasn't listening. Reluctantly, Bree followed him around the house. Andy came too.

The gate of the back fence was open, and Carl led them into the yard. It was prettier than the front yard. Someone had clearly tended it with great love. Two children sat on swings, twisting slowly, making circles in the dirt at their feet, staring at their shoes. Bree had the sudden overwhelming feeling that they were the bereaved. They looked up when the trio came into the yard.

"Hello," Andy said.

"Hey." The little boy looked up, and the look on his face said he was soul-weary of meeting new people. "Food goes inside."

"Uh . . . we don't have food."

"Not them," Carl whispered. "Right back here."

He headed toward a garden with tall hedges at the back of the yard. Over the tops of the hedges, Bree saw a gazebo. Carl took them straight toward it. They stepped around the hedges and into a garden. A man sat alone in the gazebo, his eyes toward the back of the yard.

Carl slowed his steps, but kept heading toward the man. Bree knew what was wrong before she ever looked into his eyes. He was the widower. His wife, the mother of his children, was dead.

The man heard them coming and slowly turned around.

Flash.

She saw him running through the hospital, searching each face and each bed for his wife, screaming out her name, asking if anyone had seen her.

Flash.

She had died in the earthquake, just as they thought. She had been buried in a building just like Bree had. Tears filled her eyes, but she managed to speak.

"Sir, I'm so sorry about your wife."

He looked up at her. "Do I know you?"

"No, but I'm Bree Harris, and this is Andy Hendrix and Carl Dennis. We were all buried in rubble when our building collapsed—" She started to cry and couldn't go on.

He rubbed his eyes. "My wife was pulled out two days ago. She was probably dead the moment the quake happened. Her skull was crushed. She never even knew what hit her." He wiped his eyes and got to his feet. "I'm Lawrence Grisham. How do you know about my wife?"

Andy introduced them. "You're going to think this is weird, but the Lord led us here today. He thought you needed help."

"I do." The man broke down. "I can't do this. I've never been the one people stared at and felt sorry for at a funeral. My poor kids. Those people in my house—I don't know them. They were my wife's friends from church. But I never went with her. Oh, no, I was too busy, too preoccupied. I had better things to do." The words rang with self-hatred.

"And now all these people are here bringing dishes and food and hugs for her parents who are in the house organizing everything. I don't want to talk to those people. All I want is to turn back time just a little bit so I can tell her how much I love her, start going to church with her. That's all she ever really wanted from me, to be a church-going man. But that wasn't what I was, and I wasn't about to change." His face twisted in despair. "What a disappointment I must have been to her."

"You could change now," Andy said. "It's not too late."

"It *is* too late." The man rubbed his hand across his mouth. "She's *gone.*"

"But the children aren't gone." Andy touched his shoulder and gazed in his eyes. "You've still got them. And all the prayers your wife prayed for you have yet to be answered. Do you believe that your wife is in heaven?"

"Absolutely. She's been in love with Jesus ever since I've known her. I fooled her into thinking I was like her before we got married, then slowly but surely I pulled the rug out from under her and showed my true colors. I don't know why she even stayed with me."

"Well, don't you want to see her again?"

"Of course I do, but how can I? I'm not going where she's going. If there's a God, He's probably disgusted with me. In fact, isn't there some Scripture that says He wants to vomit you out of His mouth?"

Andy shook his head. "When He said that, He was talking to Christians who were neither hot nor cold. The truth is, Christ came to save that which was lost, and that's why we're here. We're sort of the same way, seeking and saving that which is lost. And for some reason, God led us to your house today. We didn't know you from Adam, didn't know why people were milling around here, but we saw that there was a need. And the Lord just kind of led us around to the backyard here where we could find you and tell you that He loves you. He hasn't given up on you, Lawrence. You can see your wife again one day, and so can your children, if you can just believe what she believed."

Grisham got up, walked around the gazebo, and turned back toward the house. "I'm a builder, you know. I built half the houses in this neighborhood. I took a lot of pride in my work. I thought I was a great provider for my family. I thought I gave them everything they needed . . . but now I find out just how useless I was."

"Sir, how can you say that? You built a beautiful home here."

"And now my wife is gone! I'm stuck here raising the children, and I don't know what to do. I don't think I've ever been alone with them a day in my life. I love them; don't get me wrong. I just don't know what to do. My wife did it all, and it only now occurs to me how much I needed her. She was everything."

He broke down and slumped down on the bench, dropping his face into his hands. "If only I could be more like her, if I could think the things she thought, feel the feelings she felt. If I could be the kind of person she was, maybe I could raise these kids and do what I need to do by them. But that would be too much of a miracle."

Andy sat beside him. "God's in the business of miracles. Don't you understand that?"

"Then why didn't He save her?"

Bree looked at Andy, wondering how in the world he'd find the wisdom to answer that question.

But Andy wasn't daunted. "He did save her. She was taken to heaven. She's in a safe place. But God's not finished with you, Lawrence. The Lord loves you, and He has you on His mind. He's working in your life whether you can see Him or not."

The man sat there a moment, studying his hands, his forehead pleated as he tried to work it all out. Andy had the grace to let quiet settle over them.

Finally the man got to his feet again and slid his hands into his pockets. "Do you guys have a church, or what?"

"Yes, sir," Bree said, "we do. We go to the same church. It's Brotherhood Community Church over on Chapel Road."

"Well, maybe I need to visit it. I think it would be too painful for my kids to go back to their church, to sit there without their mother. Maybe we need some place new."

"I can understand that," Andy said, "but we're not here to rob churches of their members. We just want to help you."

"Do you have a service tonight?"

"Yes," Bree said, "but are you sure you want to come this soon?"

"Yes, I'm sure." His face took on a determined look. "I made some promises to God while I was sitting at the burial service, and I think it's time I started keeping them. My kids and I will be there tonight. We'll see if God will really give me another chance."

15

CARL'S FEET DIDN'T SEEM TO HAVE A DIRECTION AS they left the Grisham house, so he and the others each decided to go home and rest before church.

Bree's mother was napping when she got home, and her children were still at their friend's.

She went to her room and opened her Bible. She'd never been one to spend a lot of time poring over Scripture, but now she felt it was a missing piece in her life. And it was a piece she needed for the job God had set before her. Even so, she feared it was too late to catch up. The Lord had given her a job to do, but she had flippantly skipped the training.

She opened to Romans and turned a few pages, then her eyes fell to a highlighted passage—Romans 12. Her pastor had preached on this last week, just days before the earthquake. His sermon was about equipping the Body of

Christ and how each believer had different gifts, but all those gifts worked together.

How appropriate! And why was she surprised that the Lord had led her to this today? Smiling, she began to read.

———

The moment Carl was inside his apartment, his feet led him straight to his Bible. It lay open on his bed table, and he picked it up and took it in the living room to the couch. He sat down and turned on the lamp, then opened it to a passage he'd highlighted in yellow. Romans 12.

"I urge you therefore, brethren, by the mercies of God, to present your bodies a living and holy sacrifice, acceptable to God, which is your spiritual service of worship. And do not be conformed to this world, but be transformed by the renewing of your mind . . ."

Carl stopped reading and stared at the page, running those last few words through his mind: *Transformed by the renewing of your mind.*

He thought about those words, over and over, trying to crack the code that had always seemed like gibberish before.

And then he understood. Just because his feet were

running all over the place in his rescue operation for God, it didn't in any way mean he was better than any other Christian. And that meant his mind and heart had some growing to do.

He read on.

. . . "that you may prove what the will of God is, that which is good and acceptable and perfect. For through the grace given to me I say to every man among you not to think more highly of himself than he ought to think; but to think so as to have sound judgment, as God has allotted to each a measure of faith."

Carl got up and paced his apartment, rubbing the back of his neck. He was no super-athlete, running the hundred-yard dash from disaster to broken heart. He was just a short, skinny, bald guy, like he'd always been.

But he was chosen by God, not just to have amazing feet, but for salvation, and eternal life, and a share in Christ's own inheritance. He went back to his Bible and read on.

"For just as we have many members in one body and all the members do not have the same function, so we, who are many, are one body in Christ, and individually members one of another."

He sat back down and stared at a nail hole on his wall.

No doubt about it, the Lord was speaking to him. And with all his heart, he determined that he would listen.

———

Andy tried to sleep when he got home, but he kept looking at his Bible, lying open on the desk in the corner of his room. He was dog tired. He had stayed up all night last night, reading Scripture and trying to prepare himself for the situations the Lord would put him in today. But now he felt compelled to read and study more.

He got up and went to his desk, then looked down at the passage on the open page.

And since we have gifts that differ according to the grace given to us, let each exercise them accordingly: if prophecy, according to the proportion of his faith; if service, in his serving; or he who teaches, in his teaching; or he who exhorts, in his exhortation; he who gives, with liberality; he who leads, with diligence; he who shows mercy, with cheerfulness.

Andy frowned. A jolt went through him that the Lord was speaking to him, as clearly as if He had appeared to him. "Why did You show me this, Lord?"

He walked around his small house, processing what he'd read. "We've got these gifts and we've used them together . . . But there are other gifts, and other gifted people . . ."

His voice trailed off, and he picked the Bible up.

"Let love be without hypocrisy. Abhor what is evil; cling to what is good. Be devoted to one another in brotherly love; give preference to one another in honor."

"I will, Lord. No matter what, I will. I understand that the work doesn't stop when we lead people to You. There's more to be done." He swallowed, feeling humbled and small. "Teach me, Lord. I'm listening."

16

BREE'S AFTERNOON OF STUDY LEFT HER FEELING more equipped than ever as she went back to church for the evening service. Carl and Andy waited in the parking lot for her, and she rushed toward them.

"I feel so good! I had a great Bible study this afternoon and I'm ready to go."

"Me too." Andy grinned. "I felt like God was talking right to me."

"I had the same experience," Carl said. "It was awesome."

They started inside. The corridor was crowded with milling people, chattering and laughing before entering the sanctuary. She saw several visitors engaged in conversations with members.

A sickly looking woman with thinning hair and yellow skin met Bree's eyes.

She waited for the flash, but there was none. She glanced at the member who was talking to the woman, and hoped that she was filling the woman's needs.

Bree moved on, following Carl into the crowd, but he walked slowly, with no particular purpose. Andy walked in a brooding silence . . . just as he'd done so often before the quake.

Carl stopped and leaned back against the wall, looking around with a frown on his face. Bree stood there, waiting for him to tell her who to look at, but he was staring at the floor.

She turned and met another woman's eyes.

Nothing.

She looked at a man. A little girl. A teenage boy.

Lord, I don't see.

"Something's happened." Andy's words turned her around, and she frowned up into his somber eyes.

"Yeah, let's find some place to talk. Carl?"

He nodded, but this time he didn't lead them. He followed as Andy led them up the hall.

All the way there, Bree locked into people's gazes, trying to see with her gift, trying to understand their hearts.

But nothing happened.

Finally, they reached the same room they'd gone into the other night, and Carl turned the light on.

"I've lost the gift." They said it simultaneously, then caught their breath.

"You too?" Andy asked. "I thought it was just me."

"I'm walking aimlessly," Carl said. "My feet feel like lead."

Bree shook her head. "And I've met the eyes of a dozen people and haven't had one flash."

Carl sank down and propped his chin on the heels of his hands. "Man, what does *this* mean?"

"Maybe we blew it," Andy said. "Maybe God took our gifts away because we didn't use them well enough."

Bree couldn't believe that was true. "What more could we have done? We went until Carl's urge faded. Then I felt like God was sending us home to rest."

"Then why?" Carl asked. "Why would He give us these precious gifts, then snatch them away?"

Bree shoved her fingers through her hair and tried to think. "You know, it's crazy. When I first got this gift, it scared me to death. Remember when we came in here the other night, and our heads were spinning because we didn't know what was happening? I didn't *want* the gift. But now that I've had it and I've seen its power, I don't want to lose it."

She went to the window and looked out on one of

the parking lots. It was going to be a record crowd for a Sunday night. So many people looking for God.

"Does this mean our work is over?" Carl asked the question on a raspy breath.

Bree turned back around.

"It can't be," Andy said. "A Christian's work is never over. Ours just got started."

"But how can we do it without the gifts?" Carl's question held a note of despair. "We'll go back to being just as useless and ineffective as we were before we got them."

A knock sounded on the door, and Jim, the pastor, stuck his head in. "I saw you guys come in here. Am I interrupting anything?"

Andy got to his feet. "No, come on in, Jim."

"I just wanted to ask you guys a favor. Tonight, I plan to have a testimony time in the service. I'd love to have the three of you talk about your miracle healings and how God's been working in you ever since. Would you mind sharing that with the congregation?"

Bree shot Andy an alarmed look. Carl just kept his eyes on his toes.

"I don't know how helpful we'd be, Jim." Andy cleared his throat. "There must be someone better."

Jim laughed. "Are you kidding? Who? You're the best example I've seen of the body of Christ in action."

Carl looked up. "I could say a few words."

Bree sighed. "Yeah, me too, for what it's worth."

Andy was the last to give in. "All right. I'll think of something to say."

When Jim had left them alone, they all stood there, staring at the door.

"I can't believe I agreed to that," Andy said.

"Me either." Bree crossed her arms. "So I guess we'd better start planning what we're going to say."

Andy sighed. "Well, I guess we tell them about the healing. God didn't take that away from us, did he? My lungs and throat are fine. Carl can still walk. And you can see."

Light began to dawn in Bree's heart. "You know . . . you're right. The healing stands."

Carl got up. "And so does the fruit. God didn't revoke that, did He?"

Bree moved across the room and stood in front of both men. "Are we ungrateful, or what? Here I am feeling sorry for myself because I don't have x-ray vision, and for all intents and purposes, I'm supposed to be blinded beyond help."

"Yeah, and I probably wouldn't have walked for the rest of my life." Carl's eyes grew misty. "I feel like such a heel."

Andy laughed. "No pun intended?"

They all grinned.

"So He gave us the gifts for forty-eight hours," Andy said. "I don't think we need to feel punished because He took them back. We should feel blessed because He let us be a part of such a mighty work. And the truth is, we were all changed. I sure was."

"Yeah, me too." Bree's voice lowered to a soft whisper. "Now that I've had the chance to bear fruit, I don't think I'll ever go back to the way I was before."

"Nope." Carl took both of their hands. "I think maybe we owe God a prayer, a word of thanks, and a petition for His Holy Spirit to help us keep serving Him."

So the three of them prayed.

17

BREE'S CHILDREN MET HER IN THE SANCTUARY AND sat on either side of her in one of the front pews. Andy and Carl sat down the row from her.

As she sat there, warm gratitude washed over her that her life had been spared, that her children were fine, that her eyesight was as good as ever.

But she was different.

Thank You, Lord.

They sang and praised the Lord, then Jim launched into his sermon. Finally, he turned to the trio and asked them to come to the pulpit. As they made their way up, the congregation grew silent.

Andy took the lead. "Two days ago, the three of us were sitting in our office lounge after work, trying to get into a Bible study that was meant to be an outreach to our office. There was only one thing wrong. None of us had bothered to get the word out to the others in the office. So it was just us, and we were pretty pathetic. And then the earthquake came."

Emotion caught his words and twisted his face, and he cleared his throat. "We were buried together, under three floors of rubble. We thought we were going to die, but God had other plans." He broke down and couldn't go on.

Carl stepped up to the microphone. "A fire broke out near Andy, and he had a lot of smoke inhalation, wrecking his vocal cords and his lungs. Bree had something shatter into her eyes, and she was blinded. My legs were crushed into what felt like a zillion pieces." He held out his arms. "We have documented proof. X-rays. Paramedics who treated us. Doctors and nurses. But look at us now."

A slow applause started over the room, and Carl stepped back from the pulpit. Bree took the baton.

"Once we were healed, we felt we needed to give God our best in return, so we've been going out for the past two days, under the power of the Holy Spirit, and He took us to places we ordinarily wouldn't have gone. We met an elderly woman who'd had a stroke and was lying helpless on the floor. We met a woman who'd been abused by a violent husband. We met an alcoholic. We met a man whose pregnant wife had just lost their baby. We met a family who'd just buried their wife and mother."

She looked out over the congregation, and saw Sarah Manning sitting among several members. She was getting more comfortable with the crowds. Dr. John Fryer sat on the second row, his Bible open in his lap. Sam Jones sat near the back, all alone. And Lawrence Grisham sat in the center of the room, his somber children on either side of him.

"I'm different now." Bree struggled to keep her voice steady. "I don't just look past your faces anymore. I see *into* them. I see people who are hurting, people who need help, people who need the Lord. I can't get to them all, and neither can Carl or Andy. We did a lot together, but we need help. We need *your* gifts, all of them."

Andy nodded and stepped up to the mike again. "This morning, the Lord led me to a passage in Romans 12."

Bree caught her breath and gaped at him. That was what she had read!

"I don't believe it," Carl whispered next to her. "I read that same passage."

Andy opened his Bible and started to read. "'For just as we have many members in one body and all the members do not have the same function, so we, who are many, are one body in Christ, and individually members one of another.' I think He wanted us to tell you that we have the gifts we need, as long as we all use them together."

Bree's eyes were full of tears when she moved next to Andy. "We all have gifts," she said. "Every one of us who's in Christ. Supernatural gifts, powered by the Holy Spirit."

Carl moved to stand on the other side of Andy. "There are lots of people out there hurting. Even before the earthquake, they were all around us. We just have to start looking . . . seeing . . . listening . . . going . . . telling . . ."

"Since the earthquake, it's going to be worse," Andy said. "People need the Lord more than ever, and that means they need us. Pastor Jim told us that he wanted us to have a spiritual triage unit here, where the wounded and broken-hearted can come for help and healing. *This* should be the place where people know they'll find Jesus."

The crowd sprang to their feet, applauding the task before them . . . and the One who had equipped them to fulfill it.

18

WHEN THE SERVICE ENDED, THE TRIO FOUND
themselves surrounded by members who wanted
to help with the spiritual triage, who just needed someone
to point them in the right direction.

Bree saw Sam Jones—the man whose wife had lost
their baby—through the crowd, quietly waiting to talk to
them. Bree excused herself from the conversation she was
engaged in and made her way to him.

"Hi, Sam. It's good to see you back tonight."

He nodded. "Yeah. Who would have thought I'd go to
church twice in one day?"

"Maybe soon you can bring your wife."

He smiled. "That's what I wanted to talk to you
about." He slid his hands into his pockets and swallowed
hard. "I was wondering if you guys would mind coming
home with me to talk to my wife tonight? She's there with

her sister, and she's still really depressed. She needs some hope . . . that maybe she'll see our baby again someday. That she'll get through this. That there's light in the darkness."

"Of course we'll come," Bree said. "Just let me tell the guys."

He blinked back the moisture in his eyes. "Thanks, Bree."

She cut back through the crowd, and as she did so, someone caught her arm. She turned and saw Camille Jackson, a long-time member who'd buried her six-year-old daughter a year ago, after a tragic car accident. "Hi, Camille."

Camille's mouth trembled. "Bree, I know you're busy, but I was so moved by what you said tonight. And I want to help. I've been steeped in grief for the past year, but there were dear church members who helped me through it. And now I'm ready to help somebody else."

Bree's spirit swelled. The Holy Spirit was at it again.

"One of you mentioned that you'd ministered to a man whose pregnant wife had lost her baby. I was thinking that maybe I could help with that."

Bree's heart tugged between laughter and tears. "Oh,

Camille. We're going to talk to her tonight. Would you come with us?"

Her face slowly brightened, and her lips stretched into a smile. "Yes, of course I will. Let me go tell my family."

Bree began to laugh as she watched Camille hurry back through the crowd.

"What's so funny?"

Dabbing her eyes, she turned to find Andy behind her. "The Holy Spirit is still doing supernatural works. He doesn't need us to have superhuman skills." She swallowed and drew in a deep breath. "Andy, we have an appointment tonight with Sam Jones's wife and sister-in-law. And Camille Jackson is coming with us."

⌗

They found Sharon Jones curled up in a recliner with a blanket over her. Shadows made half circles under her eyes, and grief seemed to have cast a pale pallor over her skin.

She wasn't in the mood for company. Her sister, Shelly, bustled around trying to make the home hospitable as the four of them filed in behind Sam and squeezed together on the couch.

Sam knelt next to her. "Honey, I know you don't feel

like talking, but I'm worried about you, and I think these people can help."

Andy leaned forward and cleared his throat. He had rehearsed his speech all the way over, but as he opened his lips to speak, Camille jumped in.

"Sharon, I lost my little girl a year ago. I think I know something of what you're going through."

Sharon straightened instantly, and that glazed look in her sad eyes faded. Her eyes locked onto Camille's face. "You did? How old was she?"

"She was six. She was hit by a car when she ran out of the yard to chase a ball." Camille had trouble getting the words out, and the pain on her face reflected that on Sharon's.

Sharon nodded. "People think that since my baby hadn't been born, since I hadn't held him alive in my arms, hadn't heard his voice, hadn't lived with him at home, that it wasn't like losing a real child."

"I don't think that," Camille whispered. "He was your baby, and you had your heart invested in him. You felt every kick, every movement. You heard his heart beating at every doctor visit."

Sharon started to cry. "I saw him sucking his thumb on the ultrasound."

Camille wiped her own tears. "I know. He was your son, and you're going to hurt for a long time."

Sharon brought the blanket up to cover her face as she wilted. Camille got up and knelt beside Sharon's chair, stroking her hair. "Are you going to have a funeral for your baby?"

Sharon sucked in a sob and looked at her husband. "My mother thinks it's a bad idea. That it would be too painful. That it would drag things out. But I want to have one. I want to honor his little life. I want to have a place I can go . . ."

"You could still have one," Camille said. "I think it would be nice. I think it would help you a lot. I'll help you plan it if you want."

Andy looked at Bree and Carl, and Bree understood his silent message: They weren't really needed here. There was little they could add. Camille was the one Sharon needed now.

When the time was right, they left Camille talking to Sharon, and Sam walked them to the door. "I don't know how to thank you. She's been closed up ever since it happened. I didn't even know she wanted a funeral. For a stranger to come here and love her like that, to bond with her in such a way . . . I just don't know what to think."

"Think the obvious," Andy said. "Think that the Lord loves you and Sharon so much that He sent the only person in our church who knew exactly what to say."

As they got back into the car, all three of them still struggled with the emotion constricting their throats. Finally, Andy managed to speak.

"You know, I went there with every intention of sharing the plan of salvation with her. Of closing the deal. Helping them pray the prayer. But the Holy Spirit taught me something I didn't expect."

"Me too," Bree said. "He taught us that we have to love first. That's what hurting people respond to."

Carl nodded. "It doesn't take fancy-shmancy sales tactics for people to come to Christ. They'll be drawn to Him automatically if we just love them. Who isn't drawn by love?"

19

SEVERAL OF THE CHURCH MEMBERS HAD EXPRESSED a desire to help May by cleaning up her house, stocking her cabinets, cooking some meals, and doing repairs on her house, so the trio headed to the hospital to ask her for the key. They were still pensive and quiet as they rode the elevator to her floor.

May's door was pulled almost shut, so Bree raised her hand to knock. But then she heard voices in the room and pushed the door slightly open to see if she was interrupting anything.

Dr. John Fryer sat next to May's bed, a Bible in his lap, reading from the book of Matthew. Sarah sat on the other side of the bed, holding the old lady's hand, and soaking in every word.

Bree knocked.

"Come in, come in!" May grinned at the trio. "All my new friends. The Lord is so good."

The sight of three to whom they'd ministered, ministering now to each other, filled Bree with such poignant feelings that she didn't trust her voice. "How are you, May?"

May reached up to hug her. "I'm wonderful. How could I not be?"

Andy and Carl hugged her too. "We don't want to interrupt this Bible study," Andy said. "But May, some of the church members wanted to bring food to your house and do some cleaning and repair work. We wanted to get your permission."

"Well, of course. Those dear people. They must have known I'd be going home tomorrow."

"Tomorrow?" Bree looked at Dr. John.

"I'm releasing her tomorrow, since I know that Sarah's going to be there to help her at home. She'll have to come back every day for physical therapy, but Sarah has committed to getting her here."

Sarah smiled. Her countenance was so different than what they'd seen in her just days earlier. "I'll take real good care of her."

"I know you will," Bree said.

Carl clapped his hands. "Well, that means that the food and help is coming in the nick of time. Would you give us a key so we could let them in tonight? Some of the members are all set to get busy."

May smiled over at Sarah. "I gave my key to Sarah, but she could go with you and let you in. Sarah, you run along with them, honey, and you supervise. One of us needs to be there to thank those darling folks."

Sarah left with them, her still-bruised face glowing. They drove over to May's house and saw that several cars already waited in front of her yard. Sarah let them in and accepted a hug from each person as they bustled in, joy and peace pulsating from them as they set about to work for the Lord by loving Sarah and May.

Bree, Carl, and Andy worked until after eleven that night. They were the last to leave, but as they looked around at the house that had been so dusty and drab before the church members had cleaned it up, they knew it would provide a sweet welcome home to May tomorrow. Sarah bustled around as if she'd already made herself at home, excited that she could now begin to pass the love she'd found on to someone else.

Bree was sure the guys were as tired as she by the time they left the house. As they got into the car, they saw headlights approaching them. The car slowed down next to theirs, and Andy looked in the window.

Lawrence Grisham, the man who'd buried his wife earlier that day, sat behind the wheel. "I was hoping I'd catch you. After church tonight, I heard about the lady who lives here. Some of the members were making plans to help her. I would have come sooner, but it took me a long time to get the kids to bed tonight. Their grandparents are at the house now, so I wanted to run over and offer some help."

Bree shot Carl an amazed look.

"That's really great of you," Andy said. "But we're about finished here. We stocked the kitchen, and several of the ladies brought casseroles and stuff. And we gave the house a real thorough cleaning."

Lawrence nodded. "Well, I thought of something I could do. I'm a builder, you know. I thought I'd come over here with my crew tomorrow and make the house wheelchair accessible. I heard the woman's paralyzed on one side, so she'll be in a wheelchair for a while."

Andy stood up straight and looked back at the two of them. Bree and Carl both began to cry.

Lawrence seemed puzzled by their reaction, so he shifted his car into park and got out, peering at them over the hood. "Did I say something wrong?"

Bree shook her head. "No, not at all." She went around

the car and hugged the man. "I'm just so amazed at the way God works."

She felt his body shake as he hugged her back.

"I was just thinking the same thing," he whispered.

20

CARL WAS QUIET AS HE PULLED INTO BREE'S driveway, and Andy leaned up on the seat and patted her shoulder.

"It's been fun, guys," Bree said. "I'll never forget the things we've done these last few days."

"I know," Andy said. "I'll be changed forever."

Carl set his wrist on the steering wheel and looked at a spot on his windshield. "I miss my gift, though. I felt so anointed there for a while. I was so full of purpose."

Andy sighed. "We still have purpose, Carl. And we *are* anointed."

"We are," Bree agreed. "We're chosen, and God has given us work to do. It was really great having God work through us like that. But you know something? I've felt God working through us tonight too, even since our gifts went away. He did things just as mighty and amazing as

321

He did when I could see with His eyes, or when Carl walked with His feet, or when Andy spoke with His tongue."

Andy started to laugh softly. "And the best part was seeing Him work like that in the rest of our church. Everyone having a purpose. Every purpose working together."

"And the fruit bearing fruit."

Bree shifted on the seat so that she could look Andy fully in the face. "We can't go back to the way we were before. I don't ever want to ignore all those needy people around me again. I don't want to be useless anymore."

"Me, either," Carl said. "I've devoted my feet to the Lord from this point on. I'm going where I'm told. Like Isaiah 52:7 says, 'How lovely on the mountains are the feet of him who brings good news, who announces peace and brings good news of happiness, who announces salvation, and says to Zion, "Your God reigns!"'"

Bree squeezed Carl's arm. "I'm going to devote my feet to Him too. And I'm going to try to keep seeing with His eyes."

"'Blessed are the eyes which see,'" Andy said. "Luke 10:23. You know what I'm going to do? I'm going to keep studying my Bible, so I can be ready in season and out of season. So that I can know God's truths well enough to speak it boldly."

"Let's all vow to do that," Bree said.

"From now on," Carl agreed, "let's be ready to speak the praises of God."

Andy nodded. "Just like Zacharias did in Luke 1:64."

"We may have lost our gifts," Bree said. "But we're still so gifted because of Christ and all He's given us. And when we go back to work and we start trying to invite people to our Bible study again, I think it'll be different this time. This time, we'll be using the power we have in the Holy Spirit. Loving them, filling their needs, attracting them to what we are in Christ." She grinned. "This time we won't leave it all up to e-mails and brochures."

"I'm with you." Carl reached out to take her hand. "We're a team."

Andy put his hand over both of theirs. "All for One, and One for All. That's God's plan for His Body."

"What a plan it is," Bree whispered. "What an awesome, amazing plan."

READING GROUP GUIDE

1. Merriam Webster's Dictionary defines "ministry" as "a person or thing through which something is accomplished." Applying that definition to the Christian faith, I would add that Christian ministry is "a person or thing through which something is accomplished to further Christ's kingdom." What have you done lately to further the kingdom of Christ?

2. In your church, are there two groups—those who serve and those being served? Which group are you in?

3. What are some excuses people use for not getting involved in ministry?

4. Some believe the paid ministers in your church are the ones who should do all the work in furthering the Kingdom. Read Ephesians 4:11–12. What does Paul say the ministerial staff are supposed to do? Who is supposed to do the actual "work of service"?

5. List the attributes of those in your church who seem to do everything. For instance, are they compassionate? Are they merciful? Do they have special skills? What makes them better suited for ministry than others? Are they really better suited, or are they just more willing?

6. Read Romans 12, then list the gifts in this passage. Do your gifts fit into any of these categories?

7. What crises or trials in your life might have prepared you for helping others?

8. What would a "spiritual triage" look like in your church?

9. Are there examples in your church, or in your area of ministry, where you've seen your fruit bearing fruit?

10. What attributes in your personality or skill sets could help further the kingdom of Christ?

11. At the end of your life, what would you like to have accomplished? Write an obituary of your life, the way you'd like for it to read. Then ask God to help you live that kind of life.

Also from Terri Blackstock

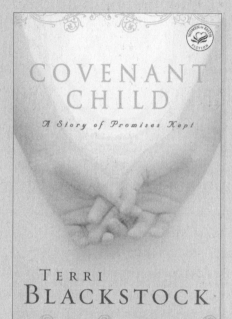

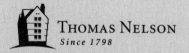

ONE

There's a question that haunts me in the blackest hours of night, when wasted moments crowd my dreams and mock the life I know. The question is this: How could a child born of privilege and promise grow up with nothing?

I was Somebody when I was born. Lizzie, my twin, says we were heiresses all along. "Our grandfather was a billionaire," she says. "Just think of it, Kara!" There were newspaper articles about us when we were three. They called us the "Billion Dollar Babies."

But these Billion Dollar Babies wore Goodwill hand-me-downs. We ate dry cereal most nights for supper, right out of the box, picking out the raisins to save for our school lunches the next day. In my memory, we never formally observed a birthday, because no one around us considered that day worthy of celebration. We were worthless no accounts to most of the people in town.

But all along we had an inheritance that no one told us was ours.

I sometimes try to remember back to the days before we were three, but my memories are tainted with the lies I've been taught and the pictures I've seen. I can't quite sift out real recollections from my faulty assumptions, but I do know that the things I've laid out here are true. Not because I remember them, but because I've studied all the sides, heard all the tales, read all the reports . . . and a few things have emerged with absolute clarity.

The first thing is that my father, Jack Holbrooke, was the son of the Paul Holbrooke, who did something with microchips and processors, things I can't begin to understand, and amassed a fortune before he was thirty. My father, Jack, got religion in his teens and decided he didn't want to play the part of the rich son. He became a pilot instead, bought a plane, and began flying charter flights and giving lessons. He disowned himself from the Holbrooke money and told his father that, instead of leaving any of it to him in his will, he preferred that he donate it to several evangelical organizations who provided relief and shared the gospel to people all over the world.

My grandfather tolerated his zeal and noted his requests, then promptly ignored them.

My mother, Sherry, was a teen runaway, who left Barton, Mississippi, at fifteen to strike out on her own. She wound up living with a kind family in Jackson, and she got religion, too. She met my father in Jackson, when he put an ad in the paper for some office help at his hangar, and they fell in love around the time she was nineteen or so. They got married and had Lizzie and me less than a year later.

She was killed in a car wreck when we were just weeks old.

Our father raised us himself for the next three years. I've seen pictures of him, and he looks like a kind, gentle man who laughed a lot. There are snapshots of him kissing us, dunking us like basketballs in his father's pool, chasing us across the lawn of the little house we lived in, reading us books, tucking us in. There are three birthday photos of our father lying on the floor with two cake-smeared redheads tearing into boxes of Barbies and Cabbage Patch dolls.

Sometimes I close my eyes and think hard, trying to bring back those moments, and for a while I convince myself that they are not just images frozen on paper, but they're live events in my head somewhere. I even think I can smell that cake and feel my father's stubbled face against mine. I can hear his laughter shaking through me and feel his arms holding me close.

But in truth, my memories don't reach that far back.

I don't even think I remember Amanda. Lizzie says she has more impressions of her than memories, that the snapshots just bring those impressions into clearer focus. I guess that's true with me, too.

But I wish I could remember when she met our father and us, how she wound up being his wife, how she was widowed and robbed of her children, and how she spent her life trying to keep a promise she had made to him . . . and to us.

But, according to Lizzie, truth is truth, whether it lies in your memory banks or not. So I'll start with Amanda's story, the way it was told to me, because it is very much the beginning of mine.